"Nina, why did you put a lock on your door?"

"I just felt like it."

Nina had begun to rock, just slightly forward and back, like a person impatient to get away.

"You have a knife in your nightstand," Zoey said.

"What the hell were you doing in my nightstand?" Nina shouted, horrified.

"Nina, something is scaring you."

"*You're* scaring me, Zo, going through my stuff."

"What's going on?"

"Will you shut up and just drive?" Nina snapped viciously.

Zoey recoiled. She had known Nina nearly all her life and had seen every mood she had. This was not part of any normal mood. This was something else.

MAKING OUT #3

Nina won't tell

KATHERINE APPLEGATE

Originally published as *Boyfriends Girlfriends*

AN AVON FLARE BOOK

Grateful acknowledgment is made for the use of the floorplan ×2690, provided by Home Planners, Inc. from *The Essential Guide to Traditional Homes*, © 1993.

Originally published by HarperPaperbacks as *Boyfriends Girlfriends*

AVON BOOKS, INC.
1350 Avenue of the Americas
New York, New York 10019

First Avon Flare Printing: August 1998

AVON FLARE TRADEMARK REG. U.S. PAT. OFF. AND IN OTHER COUNTRIES,
MARCA REGISTRADA, HECHO EN U.S.A.

Printed in the U.S.A.

WCD 10 9 8 7 6 5 4 3 2 1

For Michael

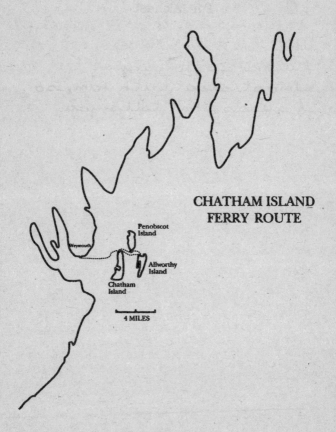

CHATHAM ISLAND
FERRY ROUTE

Penobscot
Island

Weymouth

Allworthy
Island

Chatham
Island

4 MILES

Zoey Passmore

Who do I think is sexy? That's easy. I mean, Lucas, obviously. I almost slept with him, so I guess that tells you something.

Of course, the circumstances were pretty unusual. His dad was going to kick him out of the house and ship him off to Texas, which, in case geography isn't your best subject, is a long way from Maine. Anyway, we were at that point where you think, _Oh my God, am I actually going to do this?_ Then Claire showed up and straightened everything out with Lucas's dad and, well, the moment was past.

1

I'm grateful to Claire for her timing. Definitely. At least I think I am.

I'm pretty sure that Lucas isn't.

Still, I have to be honest and say yes, I think Lucas is sexy. Very sexy. Of course, so is Scott Wolf, and I'm not going to sleep with him anytime soon, either.

Claire Geiger

Hmm. That's a more complicated question than it sounds. There are lots of guys who are definitely very good-looking who I don't find sexy. Marky Mark comes to mind. Or Scott Wolf and Antonio Sabato, Jr. I mean, pretty, yes. But sexy? On the other hand, there's someone like Jared Leto. Not handsome, but kind of sexy.

Ideally, you want a guy who combines both. Lucas was both. He was my boyfriend a long time ago. Benjamin was both, too. He was my boyfriend until very recently. Jake? Hmm. Jake. He's different. Not as

cute as Benjamin, not as obviously
sexy as Lucas.

Still, I'm strangely attracted to him.
Maybe because he's decided to blow
me off. Maybe because he doesn't
want anything to do with me. Maybe I
just like a challenge. Maybe that's
what I think is sexy.

Aisha Gray

You hear some people talk about chemistry. Like there's some automatic, out of control thing involving pheromones and hormones that just happens between two people. Blame it all on the 'mones. But I think that's too easy. That's all just an excuse for people who don't want to take responsibility for their own feelings.

Personally, I think what's sexy is a guy who shares your same interests and who treats you with respect. He has to be smart and have a good sense of humor. And be ambitious.

All of which describes Christopher. Which is why it was sensible and reasonable for me to finally go out with him even though I didn't want to at first. See, I already knew he would treat me with respect and that he had a sense of humor and was smart and ambitious. What I had to find out was if he shared my same interests.

Sure enough, as we rode the ferry home from our first date, we discovered we had a shared interest in making out. We shared this interest to the point where other passengers were covering their kids' eyes. I'd have been embarrassed except that I knew I could just blame it all on the 'mones.

Nina Geiger

Sexy? I'll tell you who's sexy. George from Seinfeld. Yeah, the short, pudgy bald guy. Oh, yes. I'd love to have a poster of him wearing nothing but briefs and a smile. Hey, hey, bay-beee.

Okay, I wasn't being serious about that. I don't think that guy is sexy. No. No, it's Paul Shaffer who gets me hot.

Still kidding.

You want the truth? The truth is, look, I don't think that way. I don't think of guys as being sexy.

Now, girls . . . .

Sorry. Okay, I'll be totally honest. Totally honestly I really, really like Benjamin. We went out on one date. At least _I_ think it was a date. He thinks I was his chauffeur for the evening. I'm surprised he didn't try to give me a tip at the end of the night.

I guess this means he doesn't think of me as exactly sexy, either. Which is fine. I don't care about that stuff; not that I'm a prude or anything. Really. It's just that what I feel for Benjamin is more spiritual. I think more in terms of us being, I don't—

know, like together in a kind of,
you know ... I'm not explaining
this well, am I? Never mind.
Next question.

One

The whistle shrieked, obliterating every other sound. The ferry strained and vibrated and churned the dark water to a cheerier blue-green. It pulled back from the dock, turning clumsily away from the already failing sun, and pointed its blunt nose across the cold, oily chop toward the island.

Nina Geiger pulled the red-and-white pack of Lucky Strikes from her purse, extracted one cigarette, and popped it in the corner of her mouth. She drew deeply on it and exhaled contentedly.

The young man on the bench behind her leaned forward over her shoulder. "Do you need a light?" A yellow plastic lighter was in his hand.

"No thanks, I don't smoke," Nina said, speaking around the cigarette. She turned to Zoey Passmore, a willowy blond seated beside her. "The guy's trying to kill me," Nina said with mock outrage.

Zoey refused to look up from her book. Nina bent forward and looked past Zoey to Aisha Gray. "What's with Zoey?"

"Studying," Aisha said with a shrug. Her eyes

Aisha held up her hand as if taking an oath. "True fact."

Nina laughed. "You're saying I can blow every test—"

"And you'll get a *B*-plus," Zoey said. "If you want an A-plus, you have to work a little harder."

Nina thought it over for a moment. "Wait a minute. How about if I tell Ms. Lehr that my self-esteem will be crushed unless I get an *A*?"

Zoey and Aisha exchanged a look.

"Damn," Aisha said.

"Never thought of that," Zoey admitted.

The ferry was up to top speed now, heading across the harbor with its cargo of high school students, homeward-bound shoppers loaded with bags, and early commuters hunched over folded newspapers. The trip to Chatham Island took twenty-five minutes.

Nina saw her sister, Claire, come up from the lower deck. She appeared first as a head of glossy, long black hair rising from the stairwell, then step by step revealed the body that had half the guys at Weymouth High quivering. *Okay, three quarters of the guys*, Nina corrected herself.

Claire glanced at Nina, then looked away, searching the deck uncertainly for a place to sit. Nina felt a momentary twinge of sympathy but suppressed it. Claire could take care of herself.

Jake McRoyan was leaning against the forward railing, looking thoughtful and distant, his big football player's shoulders hunched forward. Zoey's brother, Benjamin, was toward the back with his

12

earphones on, staring sightlessly ahead through his Ray Bans and taking an occasional bite from a Snickers bar.

Poor Claire, Nina thought, without too much pity. Trying to find a safe, neutral place to sit, somewhere between her two ex-boyfriends and her sister.

Zoey nudged Nina in the side. She too had caught sight of Claire. "Come on," Zoey said. "It won't kill you to be nice to your sister."

Nina made a face. Zoey was a hopelessly nice person. But then, Zoey had spent her life growing up with kind, considerate, decent Benjamin as her only sibling, while Nina had grown up under the ruthless tyranny of Perfect Claire. Ice Princess. Holder of the Record for Early Breast Development. Claire the Zit-proof. Claire of the perfect taste in clothing who had never once worn anything to school that caused large numbers of people to wince and turn away. Claire who must have sold her soul to the devil because she certainly didn't have one that Nina had ever—

"Come on, Nina," Zoey said in a chiding voice that Nina hated.

Nina growled at Zoey. Then she called out, "Oh, Clai-aire."

Claire came over, looking reserved as always and a little skeptical. "Yes?"

"Would you like to join us?" Nina said, using her fingers to squeeze her mouth into a happy smile.

Claire rolled her eyes. "It's come to this. You're actually feeling sorry for me."

13

"No, we're not," Zoey said quickly.

"Yes, we are," Nina told her sister. "No one's ever seen you looking pathetic and lost and boyfriendless before."

Claire sat down beside Nina. "So, of course, you're enjoying it," she said dryly.

"No, we're not," Zoey said sincerely.

Aisha made a so-so gesture with her hand.

"You bet we're enjoying it," Nina said. "At least I was."

"How are things between you and Jake?" Zoey asked. "I mean, we haven't really talked since . . . since that night."

Claire shrugged, her eyes uncharacteristically troubled. "I told him everything. He told me to get out."

Aisha and Zoey stared at her expectantly.

"That's it," Claire said.

"You know, you're quite a storyteller," Nina said. "You really made the moment come alive."

"I went to his room. He was asleep, so I knocked louder. He eventually woke up, and I told him the truth," Claire said simply. "I said, 'Hi, Jake, you know how for the last two years you blamed Lucas for crashing the car the night your brother was killed? Well, guess what? It's all come back to me now, and it turns out *I'm* the one who was driving. I ran the car into that tree. Surprise!' " She shook her head. The lightness in her voice had turned to bitterness. "Then he told me he never wanted to speak to me again." She paused, her eyes studying her hands. "Does that make the moment come alive for you?"

14

Nina lowered her gaze. "Sorry."

"Yeah, so am I," Claire said sharply. "Sorry about what happened two years ago, sorry I didn't remember, sorry Lucas suffered. Where is he, by the way? I could grovel for him a little."

"He's at his parole officer's. He still has to go until you guys get all the legal stuff cleared up," Zoey said.

"Excellent," Claire said. "Another thing for me to be sorry about."

"Well," Nina said, for lack of anything better to say.

"You know, we're all still your friends," Zoey said, reaching across Nina to put her hand on Claire's arm.

"Really," Aisha joined in. "What happened two years ago is ancient history. And just because it took you a week longer than it should have to decide to do the right thing, that's not going to turn us against you. It's not like we ever thought you were Joan of Arc."

"We know how hard it was for you," Zoey said. "And I know Lucas is cool with it."

To Nina's amazement, her sister actually looked touched. Claire nodded mutely and looked away. For a moment Nina was afraid Claire might actually cry. It was an unnerving possibility.

"So. All forgiven, all forgotten," Nina said cheerily. "I guess there's nothing left now but the big group hug."

Claire gave her sister a dubious look.

"Anyway, we're all friends, right?" Zoey asked hopefully. "I mean, you know, island solidarity and all."

"I am glad you guys don't hate me," Claire admitted.

"I never hated you," Aisha said. "By the time I found out what was going on, it was all over."

"*I* still can't stand you, Claire," Nina said helpfully.

Claire smiled her rare, wintry smile. "We're sisters, Nina. We're not supposed to get along. Although Dad will probably want us to try, for a while at least."

"What do you mean?" Nina asked. "He knows better."

"You know. While Aunt Elizabeth and Uncle Mark are here."

Nina felt her heart thud. The unlit cigarette fell from her mouth and rolled across the gray-painted steel deck. "What are you talking about?" she demanded.

"Didn't Dad tell you? They're doing the leaf-peeping thing through Vermont and New Hampshire, then they're coming to stay with us for a week. What is the matter with you, are you choking?"

Nina realized her hand was clutching at the collar of her shirt. She forced herself to release her grip. "I better pick up that cig," Nina said in a low voice. She bent over to retrieve the cigarette, but her fingers were trembling. She took a deep breath and sat back up.

"Are you okay?" Claire asked.

"Fine," Nina said with forced cheerfulness. "Fine."

"So," Nina's father said, smiling at Claire down the length of the elegantly set dinner table, "how come we never seem to see Benjamin over here for dinner anymore?"

Nina snickered and looked down at her plate. Claire shot her a dirty look.

"Benjamin and I have sort of gone our separate ways," Claire said.

"Well. I guess I'm always the last to know," Mr. Geiger said, grinning ruefully. Then he looked more serious. "This isn't because of . . . that whole thing, is it?"

That whole thing. Nina turned the phrase over in her mind. That's what the car accident and Wade McRoyan's death, Claire's memory blackout, Lucas's false imprisonment, and Mr. Geiger's attempt to cover up the truth was going to be called. *That whole thing.* Nicely succinct.

"No, Dad," Claire said, sipping at her soup. "It just, uh . . . sort of happened."

"Yeah," said Nina, "it turns out Benjamin's been drunk continuously for the last couple of years. He finally sobered up, realized he'd been going out with Claire this whole time, and broke up with her immediately."

"Too bad," Mr. Geiger said, sparing Nina no more than a distracted glance. "I always liked Ben. I admire the way he's been able to deal with being

17

blind. Never any whining or self-pity. Half the time you forget he can't see."

"I know, Dad," Claire said impatiently. "He's the son you never had."

"I'm just saying he's a hell of a young man," Mr. Geiger persisted.

"What do you think of Jake McRoyan?" Nina asked brightly, seizing the opportunity. Claire sent her a look that would freeze lava.

Mr. Geiger shrugged. "Good kid, I guess. Stays out of trouble, from what I hear. His father's a sensible businessman, does a good job running the marina. Why, are you seeing him?"

"No, not me," Nina said.

"Nina's only sixteen," Claire said sweetly. "She's not really interested in guys yet, even though every other junior in the school is."

The barb struck home, but Nina tried to laugh it off.

Janelle, the family's housekeeper, came in and traded the soup bowls for plates of codfish and red potatoes.

"Claire said Aunt Elizabeth is maybe coming for a visit," Nina said suddenly, struggling to control the faint quaver in her voice.

Her father nodded as he chewed. "They're not positive, but it looks like it. Which reminds me— Janelle?"

Janelle stopped at the door and turned. "Yes?"

"You'd better air out the two spare bedrooms and get them ready for the weekend, just in case."

"Ayuh," Janelle said. She was the only person

Nina had ever known who actually used the classic Maine response.

"Both bedrooms?" Claire asked.

Mr. Geiger looked embarrassed. "Sometimes when people get older, they decide it's easier to sleep in separate bedrooms. If they do come, you two will have to use my bathroom, God help me, and leave them the other bathroom."

"Better give Aunt Elizabeth the front bedroom," Nina suggested. "You know, it has the view of the lighthouse and all."

Mr. Geiger shook his head. "My sister is the early riser of those two, and the back bedroom gets the early morning light. Besides, if I don't give your uncle Mark the good room, he'll think I'm mistreating him. He's got it into his head that I don't like him. He's defensive because I've always made more money than he does."

"So what?" Nina persisted. "Who cares what he thinks? I like Aunt E. better anyway. She should have the better room. After all, she's a blood relation."

"Who cares what room they stay in?" Claire asked, wrinkling her forehead in annoyance. "What's the difference to you?"

"I'm just trying to be fair," Nina said sullenly. She finished the rest of her meal and pushed away the plate. "I think I'll pass on dessert. I have a raft of homework to do."

Nina left the dining room and climbed the stairs to the second story. The back bedroom was just to her left. Nina opened the door and looked inside. It was nicely decorated, like all of the Geiger house, but had the sterile feel of a guest room, with no personal touches or sign that it had been occupied.

She closed the door and slowly, carefully paced off the distance from that door, around the open stairwell, down the hall to her own bedroom. Sixteen paces, maybe even seventeen.

Then Nina crossed over to the other spare bedroom and looked inside. It was a nicer room, no question about it, with two tall windows looking out over the northernmost point of the island and the little lighthouse on its rocky islet.

She turned and paced off the distance back to her own door. Eight paces in a nice straight line.

That was the difference: seventeen paces, past her father's bedroom door, around the stairwell, past what should be Aunt E.'s room. Or if Uncle Mark got the front bedroom, it would mean just eight steps, in a nice straight line, passing nothing.

Nina ducked into her bedroom and stared for a while at the doorknob. It was the old-fashioned kind, made of clear glass, with a keyhole beneath that had been painted over dozens of times in the two-hundred-year history of the house. She had never seen a key. In all likelihood the key had been lost a century earlier.

She closed the door. He wasn't going to come. Her father had said it was only a possibility. Fine. She was going to assume the best: he wasn't really coming. He and Aunt Elizabeth would call up and say they just couldn't make it. That's the way it would be. That's the way it had to be.

NINA'S HOUSE

Second floor

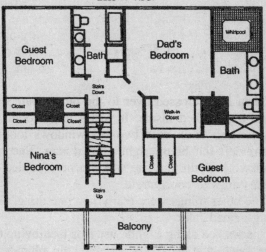

Third floor

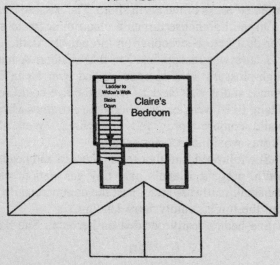

Two

Claire left the house right after dinner. She had homework to do, but she was too preoccupied by other things to concentrate.

The other things were really just one thing. One thing named Jake.

She walked along Lighthouse Road, enjoying the nice swell that was sending dramatic plumes of spray surging up and raining down noisily on the tumbled rocks of the north shore. The passing beam from the lighthouse turned a cloud of spray to silver dust before sweeping on through the dark.

Claire was disappointed in the weather. A huge high-pressure front seemed parked over New England, and it was clear as far as the eye could see. Claire liked weather, especially the extremes Maine could conjure up in fall and winter. Well, the storms would start soon enough.

She followed Lighthouse as it curved and headed south, past the island's only tiny gas station, past the small hardware store, past the commercial dock and the bright, empty ferry landing.

She hadn't really decided on her goal. She harbored some vague hope that she might run into Jake, and having accidentally, casually, run into him, that she might find a way to get him to talk. Talking was the necessary first step.

She spotted Zoey and Aisha sitting out in front of the Passmores' restaurant, sipping sodas and looking bored.

Claire hesitated. They'd all kissed and made up that morning, but still, where Zoey was, Lucas couldn't be far away. And she still wasn't ready to make small talk with Lucas Cabral.

Claire cut discreetly up Exchange Street through the candy stores and souvenir shops that catered to the summertime tourist trade. Many were already closed down for the winter, their glass fronts shuttered, doors barred, upper-story windows dark.

Getting around Zoey and Aisha without being seen would take her several blocks out of her way—assuming, as she had just admitted to herself, that her goal was Jake's house.

Was that her goal? What could she possibly do? Just walk up, knock on his door, and pretend nothing had happened? What could she say? Sorry?

The detour through town eventually brought her to Dock Street. It curved along Town Beach, a placid, underused strand of sand, crushed shell, and washed-up seaweed. In the harbor sailboats were moored, ghosts in the dark. She reached the intersection and hesitated. She could either follow the road along toward Jake's house or turn right to go out onto the breakwater. Claire stood and considered, her gaze drawn by the slowly flashing beacon that marked the end of the breakwater.

She heard his steps on the sand and gravel only after it was too late to think what she should say. She turned and saw him just as he, raising his eyes from the ground, spotted her. He was carrying a canvas bag slung over his shoulder and a can of Budweiser in his free hand.

"Huh" was all he said.

"Hi, Jake," Claire said.

He looked as if he was trying to summon up something harsh to say, but the effort went nowhere. He just shrugged and said, "Yeah, hi, Claire."

"Jake . . . I thought maybe we could talk," Claire said. It was the most clichéd thing in the world to say, but she didn't know how else to put it.

"Maybe you need to talk. I need to drink beer."

"You're just going to walk down the road drinking beer?" Claire asked, trying not to sound too much like his mother.

"Better than driving down the road drinking beer, as you should know, Claire." He laughed shortly at his joke. "Actually, I'm going to go sit at the end of the breakwater and drink beer."

Claire shot a look down the long, concrete expanse of the breakwater. The surf that had been giving the north shore a good pounding was even more forceful as it slammed against the breakwater. It was nothing that would have been dangerous to Jake . . . if he were sober.

"I wonder if I could come with you," Claire

asked. "We wouldn't really have to talk."

Jake cocked a sarcastic eye at her. "I don't know, Claire," he said. "You might *accidentally* knock me into the water. My father would be pissed. There would be no one left to carry on the proud McRoyan name."

Claire bowed her head. "I deserve that, I guess."

"No, you deserve to spend a couple of years at Youth Authority," Jake said coldly. "But that's what Lucas got. Wade got dead . . ." His voice quivered a little, but he regained control by redoubling the venom in his tone. "Lucas got jail. And Claire—the one actually driving the car—Claire got to walk away unhurt, untouched. Just a little bruise on the head, just enough so that she could claim her memory was screwed up. Lucky Claire."

He brushed past her, heading down the short connecting road to the breakwater.

"Jake," she called after him.

He marched on, seemingly oblivious.

"Jake," she cried, "don't you realize how much I care for you?"

He stopped and hung his head, as if in deep thought. Claire held her breath. Then Jake drained his can of beer, tossed it in the general direction of a trash barrel, pulled a new beer from his canvas bag, and popped it open.

"Jake, the surf is up," Claire warned. "Let me come with you."

"Go screw yourself, Claire," Jake said. He walked on, and Claire watched him. He was still moving confidently. He wasn't drunk yet. But judging by the bulk of his bag, she could tell he would be, sooner or later. And even strong, powerful swimmers like Jake could be battered to death if they fell between the irresistible force of the sea and the immovable breakwater.

Let alone when they were drunk.

She waited till he had reached the end of the breakwater and flopped down on the wet concrete, a dark, hunched creature lit only by the dim glow from the lights of town and the intermittent flash of the green warning beacon.

Claire walked halfway down the breakwater toward him, stopping well out of earshot. She sat down on a dry patch of concrete and checked her watch.

Great. So much for getting her homework done tonight. She had to spend her evening baby-sitting a guy who hated her.

Why? Claire asked herself mockingly. Why was she doing this? Like Aisha said, she wasn't Joan of Arc.

Because she didn't want anything to happen to him.

And why did she care what happened to Jake? Because she felt guilty? Because she felt she owed him?

Because she'd started to love him?

All of the above?

Jake started on his third beer and Claire lay back, looking up at the clear, star-strewn sky, and wished for a storm, or some other clear, easy answer.

"This table wobbles," Aisha complained. "You should tell your parents."

Zoey used her paper napkin to mop up the Pepsi that Aisha had spilled. "It's not the table," she explained. "It's the brick sidewalk. The bricks are uneven."

"Oh," Aisha said, looking under the table.

"Besides, you're complaining? The soda's free since you're such a good friend of the owners' daughter."

They were sitting on the sidewalk outside Passmores' at one of the restaurant's three small outdoor tables. The other two tables were empty. It was a slow night for business, and her dad and mom had both gone home for a couple of hours, leaving Christopher Shupe to deal with the kitchen and Zoey to watch the dining room and bar. Their only patrons at the moment were a man and woman who were such regulars they could pour their own beers and keep track of what they owed. From inside the restaurant came the sound of CNN on TV.

"Who's complaining?" Aisha asked. "I always like to save fifty cents."

"Fifty cents?" Zoey echoed. "In what universe? We charge a buck and a quarter for sodas. A dollar seventy-five during tourist season."

"Then I guess I'm extra grateful," Aisha said.

"Well, what have we here?"

Zoey looked up to see Christopher emerge from the doorway, wearing a white chef's jacket and stained apron over shorts.

"All the beauty and class and charm that Chatham Island has to offer," he said. "Oh, and you're here, too, Aisha."

Aisha fished an ice cube out of her drink and tossed it at him. He sidestepped easily and bent over to plant a light kiss on her lips.

"Where's Lucas?" Christopher asked.

"The ferry's not in yet," Zoey said.

"Oh, man," Christopher groaned. "Are you telling me it's not seven yet? This night is dragging. I've done all the prep I can do; I changed the oil in the fryer and mopped out the walk-in. If biz doesn't pick up, your dad will have to cut back my hours."

"It's always slow in the fall," Zoey said reassuringly. "When the cold weather sets in, we'll get more business because people don't want to drag over to the mainland."

"Christopher hasn't done the Maine winter experience yet," Aisha said, grinning at Zoey.

"Oh, that's right. You may want to get some long pants," Zoey said. "It gets slightly chilly." She saw the bright running lights of the ferry coming around the breakwater, twinkling through the masts of the sailboats anchored in the harbor. "Here it comes," she said. She strained, hoping for an early glimpse of Lucas. But he didn't appear until several minutes later, after the ferry had docked.

He came sauntering across the bright square, heading straight up the street toward his house, unaware that Zoey was waiting for him.

"You want me to get him for you?" Christopher asked.

"Would you mind?" Zoey asked. "I would, but I'm not supposed to leave the immediate vicinity of the cash register."

Christopher ran off and quickly caught up with Lucas. They came back at a leisurely walk.

Christopher was the taller and heavier of the two, by an inch and a few pounds. He moved with a bouncy, restless energy, like an overgrown puppy who couldn't wait to chase something. He always seemed to be checking out everyone and everything around him, like a serious shopper sizing things up in a hurry, analyzing, pricing, wondering how much he could carry. It was easy for Zoey to see why Aisha liked him—boundless self-confidence, intelligence, a sense of humor.

Lucas moved with more economy, conserving his energy. His interest in the world around him was more selective. His eyes roamed, considered, dismissed, and went on to the next thing. Yet there was always the sense that he was on guard, only pretending to be relaxed. He often seemed serious, as if he were distracted by important things that only he knew about. His smile, when it appeared, was a slow, rueful thing that made him seem, at least to Zoey's eyes, utterly irresistible.

"All the looks and style and manly muscle on Chatham Island," Aisha said as soon as Christopher and Lucas were within earshot. "Oh, and I see you're back, too, Christopher."

Christopher laughed and wagged his finger at her.

"Hey, Zoey, guess what?" Lucas said. "I'm free. My parole officer said it was obvious the conviction would be expunged, so he doesn't want me wasting his time anymore."

"That's great," Zoey said happily as she jumped up and threw her arms around Lucas.

"Expunged." Christopher tried out the word. "Excellent word. I'll have to use it sometime. Expunge me."

Lucas kissed Zoey's lips, sending a thrill through her that hadn't diminished at all in the weeks they had been together. After a few seconds she pulled away, jerking her head meaningfully toward Aisha and Christopher.

"You want us to cover our eyes?" Aisha suggested.

"I think they make a cute couple," Christopher said sarcastically. "They're both so sweet."

"Chew me, Christopher," Lucas said mildly. He closed his eyes and kissed Zoey again.

"You know," Aisha said thoughtfully, "you two do make such a nice-looking couple. And with homecoming and all, well, I think you'd be a cinch for homecoming king and queen. It would have such a nice symbolic thing going. I mean, Lucas *has* come home. All you need is like a dozen votes to nominate you."

"I don't think I'd be a contender," Zoey said, pulling away from Lucas. "Remember when I ran for student council and came in fourth behind Beavis?"

"You beat Butthead," Aisha pointed out encouragingly.

"I'll have to remember to put that on all my college applications," Zoey said, laughing. "Anyway, I'm not one of those people who enjoy repeated humiliation."

"Oh, come on," Aisha said. "Cartoon morons aren't even eligible for homecoming queen, so you have a pretty good chance."

"Excuse me," Lucas said firmly. "But I'm not going to be king or queen of anything."

"You're just being modest," Christopher teased. "You know you want the job. The power, the glory."

"Uh-huh," Lucas said. "Check the weather forecast. The day they announce that hell has frozen over, I'll be glad to run for homecoming king."

In Zoey's room Lucas leaned into the dormered window and checked the quote wall where Zoey stuck bits of wisdom on yellow Post-it notes.

"Anything new and deep?" he asked lightly.

Zoey smiled a little self-consciously. Jake had never shown much interest in her quotes when he was her boyfriend. And her friends just dismissed it as a harmless quirk of character.

Lucas scanned the latest Post-it.

The world is a comedy to those who think; a tragedy to those who feel.

He stood back. "And which are you?"

Zoey ran her hand through her hair and shrugged. "That's what I've been trying to figure out."

Lucas put his arms around her waist and pulled her to him. He kissed her lightly. "Did you feel that or think about it?" he asked.

"That?" Zoey asked. "That I thought about."

Lucas kissed her again, more deeply, till she closed her eyes and wrapped her arms around his neck and held him closer still.

"That I felt," she said in a husky voice.

"So it was a tragic kiss?"

"At least it wasn't a comic kiss," she pointed out.

He looked at her skeptically. "What would a comic kiss be?"

She drew him down to her again, pressed her lips to his, and made a sudden loud, razzing noise.

Lucas jumped back, laughing and rubbing his mouth.

"That would be a comic kiss," Zoey said. She let Lucas pull her onto her bed, and they lay back on her comforter side by side.

"That's the kind of dumb joke I'd expect from Nina," Lucas said. "You know, if she liked guys."

Zoey rolled onto her side. "What do you mean by that? Nina likes guys."

Lucas shrugged. "You know. I just meant Nina doesn't go out much. Even back before I went away, she wasn't into guys."

"Well, she's not gay or anything," Zoey said defensively, "if that's what you're thinking. Not that it would matter if she were. At least, it wouldn't matter to me. Besides, back then she was just fourteen. Lots of girls don't date when they're fourteen."

"Has she dated since then?"

Zoey sat up on the edge of the bed. "Once or twice, maybe," she said, feeling uncomfortable.

"She's a very pretty girl," Lucas said. "Not that I've ever looked at her in that way. I mean, when she took Benjamin to the concert down in Portland and she was all dressed up, I was surprised."

"I don't think Nina thinks she's attractive," Zoey said. "She's always going on about how Claire used up the family's quota of breasts and good looks. I think Nina just has an inferiority complex about her sister."

"I'll bet tons of guys would go out with Nina if she would give them a chance. But you know how she is. She's a ball-buster."

"A ball-buster?" Zoey repeated the phrase distastefully. "What exactly is that supposed to mean?"

"Nothing," Lucas said innocently. "Just, you know, any guy who might ever want to ask her out would be afraid she'd shoot him down."

"She probably would," Zoey admitted. Nina's total lack of a love life was a topic Zoey had always instinctively avoided. Aisha had asked her about it once and gotten quickly chopped off. "I don't like prying into other people's private lives," Zoey said.

"You are her best friend," Lucas said. "Doesn't she pry into yours?"

Zoey found herself grinning.

"What?" Lucas asked.

"Nothing," Zoey said, but her grin spread. "Okay, you're right. She does pry. She asked about you versus Jake."

Lucas sat up, looking wary. "What do you mean, me versus Jake?"

"She asked, you know, private stuff."

"Like what?"

"Oh . . . you know," Zoey teased.

"No, I don't know," Lucas said, suddenly very serious in a way that made Zoey laugh. "Like what?"

"Like—you know, about how you kissed compared to how Jake kissed."

"How can you compare things like that?"

"That's what Nina was asking."

Lucas gave her a dirty look. "Are you going to tell me what she asked you?"

"It was a private conversation," Zoey said.

"It was about me," Lucas said almost desperately. "You can't just go around discussing me with all your friends, talking about . . . all that stuff."

34

"Why not? You were just trying to get me to talk about Nina."

"That's different," Lucas said dismissively. "What did you tell her?"

"Them. What did I tell them," Zoey clarified. "Aisha was there, too."

"Oh, great."

"Really, most of it was too embarrassing to repeat. You know, stuff like when we make out, do you, you know . . . and what do you do then, and what do I do, and so on. And then we were talking about . . . well, never mind."

"Uh-huh. You know, guys talk about things, too," Lucas warned.

"I'm sure you do," Zoey said indifferently.

Lucas lunged suddenly and grabbed her around the waist. He threw her down on the bed and began tickling her ribs.

Zoey squealed and tried to squirm away, but Lucas was too strong.

"Did you say I was the best?" Lucas demanded.

Zoey gasped for breath. "You're going to make me pee."

"It's your bed. Did you tell them all I was the best?" he asked again, renewing his assault.

"Yes, yes, yes!" Zoey screamed.

He stopped tickling her instantly. "All right, then," he said. His face was just inches from hers. "And what did you tell them you liked the most?"

"I can't remember," Zoey said. "Let's go over it all and I'll try to remember."

Nina

I was different when I was eleven than I am now. People who know me now probably wouldn't even recognize eleven-year-old me.

My big concern back then was would I ever get my period. Zoey already had, of course, since she's a year older, and she was going around acting like she was a WOMAN. You know the kind of thing I mean— she'd stare off into space and sigh, and when I'd ask her what she was sighing about she'd just smile and say, "Oh, Nina, you're too young to understand." And

Claire had started around age three; so...

But while I was worrying about becoming a woman, my mother was dying. It hurts to this day to think how preoccupied I was with myself while she was suffering. And I know I'll never, ever be able to think about her without wanting to cry, and feeling all over again how her death tore a hole in me that will never heal.

That's why my dad decided to send me away to stay with my aunt Elizabeth and uncle Mark. Dad said it would be good for me, change of scenery and so on. I guess it's true that my mom and

I were especially close, just the way Claire and my dad are close. Not that Claire wasn't a wreck, too. I hope I never see my sister that upset again. It's especially terrible when these cool, unemotional, in-control-type people start to lose it.

Anyway. I was gone for two months.

Soon after I came back, I had my first period. I thought it was punishment for what had happened while I was at my aunt and uncle's house. Other times I thought it was punishment because I had somehow failed to save my mother. All I knew was that it was punishment, because I was sure I deserved punishment.

Like I said, I was different when I came back home from my aunt and uncle's house. It was like the real me never did come back. I started having dreams, often the same dreams over and over again. Some are so familiar now that I have them numbered. Dream number three, dream number four, and so on. Not pleasant dreams, but the sorts of dreams that after you wake up seem to echo through the rest of the day.

I miss my mother every day.

And I miss me, the way I was before.

Three

Every morning Benjamin Passmore and the rest of the high-school-age kids from Chatham Island caught the seven-forty ferry. It arrived in Weymouth at five after eight, allowing exactly twenty-five minutes for the walk from the dock, uphill along Mainsail Drive, to the school. More than enough time.

It was a distance of about a quarter mile and involved crossing eight separate streets. Benjamin had each of the distances measured out in strides. So many from the corner of Groton to Independence, so many more to cross the street, then another number from Independence to Commerce. All in all, Benjamin had memorized more than thirty blocks since losing his sight years ago, allowing him to move confidently within all of North Harbor, Chatham Island's only town, and parts of Weymouth. Some areas he knew so well that keeping count consciously was no longer necessary. They had become as familiar as his own home. In other areas he could keep his count almost subconsciously.

But on this morning there was a complication.

Benjamin heard the high-pitched warning horns of heavy equipment backing up.

"Damn," he cursed softly. He was at the corner of Mainsail and Independence. Judging by the rumble of diesel engines and the oily smell of exhaust, he figured the equipment was probably just across the street.

Benjamin concentrated and could hear a familiar voice coming up the street behind him. Aisha. Then, as expected, he heard Zoey's voice.

He disliked relying on his little sister, but there were times when he had no choice.

When he could hear that Zoey was close enough, he smiled in her general direction and shrugged. "I think it's exactly twenty-two paces into an earthmover."

"Yeah, it looks like a water pipe broke or something," Zoey said. "It's a mess. I don't think this would be a good idea for you. Pipes and mud everywhere."

"Probably not," Benjamin agreed.

"You guys go on ahead," Zoey said. "I'll detour with Benjamin."

"I'll take him," Nina's voice said. A tractor roared, and Benjamin could now smell a whiff of natural gas.

"Hi, Nina," Benjamin said. "I didn't hear you."

"I know. Unusual, huh?" Nina said. "Come on with me. Go ahead, Zoey. You know I'm never in a hurry to get to school. We'll take the scenic route."

Benjamin put out his left arm and felt Nina insert her elbow. She had led him before and knew the routine. "Later," Benjamin said in the direction of the others.

Nina led him left, down Independence, through the busy, bustling early morning commuter crush of Weymouth. "You didn't have to do this," Benjamin said. "Zoey usually gets stuck."

"I know you don't like to ask your sister," Nina said.

Benjamin smiled. "You do, huh? How do you know that? Is that what Zoey thinks?"

"Nope. I just know," Nina said. "You always get a certain way when you have to ask her for help. Embarrassed or something."

Benjamin felt uncomfortable. "I'm not embarrassed," he said in a tone that was grouchier than he'd intended. He softened it a bit. "It's just that I don't want Zoey spending her life as my guide. She needs to live her own life."

"I know," Nina said.

"Oh, you know that too?" Benjamin said.

"Sure. We have known each other forever, Benjamin."

"Mmm. I just didn't realize you were observing me," Benjamin said. "It makes me nervous."

"You like being mysterious," Nina said.

"What is this? Nina Freud time? I should have had Zoey take me."

"Coming to a corner. Sixth Street. We have to cross here. Execute right turn."

"Okay."

"Light's red."

"I know. I can hear the traffic moving past. The cars over there"—he pointed to his left—"are waiting for the light to change. I could probably have done this on my own. It's just three sides of a square, right? Then we hook back up with Mainsail."

Nina sighed. "It's a good thing I don't wait around for you to be grateful. It would be such a long wait."

Benjamin grinned. "Sorry, kid. I am grateful."

"Come on. Curb. Can I ask you a favor?"

"How can I say no? You could just spin me around and leave me to wander through traffic."

"I don't like it very much when you call me kid. Curb, step up."

Benjamin stepped onto the curb, caught a seam of the sidewalk, and stumbled forward a bit before regaining his balance. "Hey, that was exciting." He walked along, swinging his cane in a short arc to the right but relying on his contact with Nina for truer guidance. "Why don't you like me to call you kid? I've always called you kid."

"Because I'm not a kid," Nina said a little heatedly.

"Oh. All right, if you say so. It's just that the only picture I still have of you in my mind was when I was twelve, so you were, what, nine or ten? You were a kid then. I have this image of you with your hair cut short, with barrettes. And I think you had braces."

"That's how you think of me? Braces on my teeth and really bad hair? Jeez, what a sad

43

thought,'' Nina said. ''But you've missed most of my later zit phase, so I guess it isn't all bad.''

''I have no idea what you look like now,'' Benjamin admitted. ''I have no idea how anyone's looks may have changed in the last seven years.'' He laughed to lighten the mood. ''It used to be strange when I was going out with your sister. The Claire I was making out with looked about ten in my mind. Slightly bizarre at times.''

''Fortunately for you, by the time Claire was ten she already looked like she was twenty,'' Nina muttered.

''Anyway,'' Benjamin said, fighting off a wave of sadness at the mention of Claire. They had broken up only a short while ago. He hadn't even begun to get over her. He wasn't sure he wanted to start.

''Anyway,'' Nina said, ''I stopped being a kid years ago.''

''Yeah? What exactly is the cutoff age for not being a kid anymore?''

''Eleven,'' Nina said.

Benjamin thought he detected a trace of bitterness in her tone. ''Eleven? Why eleven?''

''Good question,'' Nina said.

Yes, she was definitely sounding angry, or resentful . . . something. ''Well, I won't call you kid anymore. But it's hard for me not to see you in my mind as a kid with braces.''

''I got rid of the braces.''

''Yeah, I kind of assumed that.''

''Turn here. Come on, we have a green light, curb, step down. Yes, I have very straight teeth

44

now. I can eat corn on the cob very neatly.''

"I'll be sure to update my mental picture. Braces out, teeth in.''

"Step up. Let's blow off school and go do something fun,'' Nina said suddenly.

Benjamin laughed. "Right, Nina. Dragging me around by the elbow; that would be major fun for you.''

"I think it would be.''

"You're a sweet kid,'' Benjamin said.

"I'm not a kid,'' Nina said.

"Good morning, students. These are the morning announcements.''

Zoey glanced up at the intercom box, then over at Aisha, two aisles away. Aisha was talking to another girl, so Zoey returned her gaze to her book. It was a paperback historical romance novel of the kind she hoped someday to write. The actual book was about two inches thick, with a lurid cover depicting the heroine, spilling her plump breasts out of her décolleté dress and clutching a nearly naked man with long blond hair. But since the entire book was too big to hide easily, Zoey had torn out a thirty-page section and concealed it inside her biology textbook.

". . . I would appreciate any information on the person or persons who caused the third-floor boys' bathroom toilets to overflow . . .'' Mr. Hardcastle, the principal, droned on.

Zoey heard a noise beside her and saw Claire scuttling forward from her own desk to sit in a vacant desk behind Zoey. Zoey clapped her biology text closed.

"Too late, Zoey," Claire whispered over her shoulder. "I know you're reading one of your bodice-rippers."

"I am not," Zoey lied automatically.

"You are such a lousy liar," Claire said disgustedly. "You really shouldn't try it unless you're willing to practice a little more."

". . . On another topic, we have reexamined school policy and taken the matter up with the school board, and it remains the official policy of this school that no student may smoke cigarettes on school grounds. And this does, I repeat *does* apply to cigarettes whether or not they are lit. I hope this will put an end to . . ."

Zoey grinned. It looked as if Nina had lost another round. She heard Claire sigh.

"Is it possible to divorce your sister?" Claire muttered.

"Nina's an original," Zoey said. "You should be proud of her."

"She's just odd, Zoey. And you should be ashamed, reading crappy books like that. What would Ms. Rafanelli think if she knew you read that stuff? It would probably disappoint her. Disappoint her terribly, given the high opinion she has of you. Probably break her heart, thinking of her star pupil poisoning her mind with stories of virgins being despoiled by knights or whatever. I only hope she never discovers the truth."

Zoey turned slightly to look over her shoulder.

Claire was looking carefully innocent, a sure sign she was up to something. "Oh," Zoey said as the realization dawned on her. "You're blackmailing me."

"Duh," Claire said.

"What do you want?"

"I want to look over your notes on the English assignment. I didn't get to the reading."

"*You* didn't get your homework done and now you want to borrow mine?" Zoey looked at Claire incredulously. "Why do you care? It would take a lot more than that to mess up your *A*."

Claire looked uncomfortable. "Okay, look, you're right. But Jake didn't do his homework, either. And he's shaky in that class."

"You want me to give you my homework so you can give it to Jake?"

"I know. It almost sounds kinky somehow, doesn't it?"

Zoey turned back toward the front of the class. She could just imagine why both Claire and Jake hadn't gotten their work done. Not that it was any of her concern now. After all, she and Jake were finished, so what did she care if Claire and Jake spent the evening groping?

Or whatever it was they were doing.

The possibility made her frown. She doubted Claire was doing *it* with Jake, but again, that wasn't her business. She glanced back over her shoulder. "So I should give you my homework because you and Jake were too busy doing . . . *whatever*?"

"We weren't doing *whatever*," Claire said.

47

"The truth is, I was watching him get faced on beer at the end of the breakwater and trying to figure out if I was strong enough to drag him back out of the water if he fell in."

Zoey raised a skeptical eye. "Jake doesn't drink."

"Things change," Claire said. "I think he's really pretty messed up over all that's happened. It was probably just a onetime deal. He'll get over it. You know Jake."

"I *do* know Jake, which is why I'm having such a hard time picturing this scene."

"Okay," Claire said. "If you don't believe that, then we were making passionate love till dawn. It was magic. He made a woman of me."

Zoey grumbled under her breath and dug in her three-ring binder for the homework. She pulled it out and handed it over her shoulder. "Just have it back to me before class."

"No problem."

"You weren't, were you?" Zoey asked.

"We weren't?" Claire echoed coyly.

"You weren't," Zoey reassured herself.

". . . and nominations for homecoming king and queen must be made by the end of this school day. Once again, please do not submit the names of fictional individuals, musical performers, animals, cartoon characters, or the deceased."

Four

Halfway up the bleachers, Claire set the can of diet Coke on the plank in front of her and dropped her books beside her. Discreetly she began wiggling out of her pantyhose. If the weather was going to insist on being boringly sunny, she might as well get a little late season tan.

She balled up her pantyhose and stuck them in her purse. Then she leaned back, stretched out her legs, hiked the hem of her skirt a few inches, and kicked off her shoes.

On the grass-and-mud field, the football team was going through a set of stretching exercises. They were dressed in bulky uniforms, with their helmets on the ground beside them. Jake seemed to be moving with the elaborate care of a person with a bad hangover.

He might not have noticed yet that she was there, Claire knew, but he would sooner or later.

He'd said little when she'd caught him in the hallway between classes and handed him a hastily transcribed version of Zoey's notes. But he must have read them because later, in class, he'd correctly answered the teacher's question. And he hadn't seemed overly panicked by the snap quiz that had followed.

Claire saw him lie back on the grass and rub his eyes with the heels of his hands. Claire had been seriously drunk exactly once in her life—on the night she drove into a tree. Since then, alcohol had held no attraction for her. And as far as she knew, Jake had never been into booze, either. His sudden interest had come immediately after the dredging up of all the events surrounding his brother's death.

"Hey, Claire."

It was Aisha, climbing the bleachers nimbly with her long legs, almost making a dance of it.

"Hi, Aisha. What are you doing here?"

Aisha flopped down beside her. "Same as you— acting like a dumb female throwback who wastes her time watching guys strut around and act macho."

Claire smiled despite herself. She searched the field, then, in a far corner, spotted Christopher, who helped coach the ragtag intramural soccer team. "You can barely see him from here."

Aisha nodded. "I don't want him to think I'm here just to watch him."

"Oh."

"He has plenty of ego already."

"Then why be here at all?" Claire asked reasonably.

"Because he works about twenty different jobs, so if I don't see him while he's working, I don't see him at all," Aisha said, suddenly vehement.

"That's what happens when you go out with guys who are out of school, I guess," Claire said, not really very interested. Jake had just glanced over at her, hesitated, then looked away.

"Are you two together again, or still, or whatever the right word is?" Aisha asked, looking at Jake as he put on his helmet and formed up with the rest of the team.

"Me and Jake?"

"No, you and Tom Cruise. Of course, you and Jake."

Claire shrugged. She disliked being asked about her private life. Especially the parts of her private life she didn't entirely understand herself. "I'm not exactly sure."

"I just assumed since you're here watching him practice . . ."

Claire shifted uncomfortably. "I'm getting my legs tan."

For a while Aisha didn't say anything, and at last Claire turned around to see what she was doing. It turned out she was staring at Claire with a speculative, thoughtful expression. "What?" Claire demanded.

"Nothing," Aisha said defensively. "I was just thinking this is kind of an unusual situation for you."

Claire was determined not to ask Aisha to explain what she meant, but her resolve gave way to annoyance. "All right, spit it out, Aisha."

"I'm just saying that as long as I've known you,

it's been guys chasing after you, looking at you all lovesick. Not the other way around."

"Don't ever use a term like *lovesick* to refer to me," Claire said frostily.

"How about *unrequited*, as in unrequited love?" Aisha asked.

"Are you trying to annoy me? Because you're doing it pretty well." She settled a hard glare on Aisha.

"You shouldn't worry about what I have to say," Aisha said, unabashed. "You have bigger things to worry about."

"Like what?"

"Like here comes Jake." Aisha batted her eyelashes dramatically.

Claire snapped her gaze back and saw Jake trotting across the field toward her. Her hand went instinctively to her hair, swooping it back over her shoulders.

"I will back off to a discreet distance," Aisha said. "But not *too* discreet." She moved up several rows and a dozen feet to the left.

"What are you doing here?" Jake demanded as he came within shouting range. He took off his helmet and gave her a cold look.

"It's a sunny afternoon," Claire said. "I'm getting some sun."

Jake pointed his index finger at her. "I don't want you here. The guys on the team are getting the wrong idea."

"What wrong idea is that, Jake?"

"Look, Claire, it's over. You and me? Over.

You think I can just go on with you now that I know the truth?''

Claire considered the question seriously. ''I think you can do whatever you want to, Jake.''

''Why don't you go pick on some other guy?'' He waved his arm back toward the team. ''There are two dozen guys who would gladly go out with you. Lars over there would sell his mother to Saddam Hussein for a chance with you. Or else go back to Benjamin, not that I would wish that on Benjamin because he's a good guy. Just forget about me, all right?''

''No,'' Claire said.

He bounded up the bleachers to stand over her, his big body blotting out the sun. ''What is it? You think you have to take care of me, compensate because you killed my brother?''

''I didn't kill Wade,'' Claire said softly. ''We were all drunk. Any one of us could have been driving. If I hadn't gotten behind the wheel, Wade would have. Then who would you blame?''

Jake didn't explode the way she expected. Instead he just laughed cruelly. ''That's not what you said when everyone thought Lucas had been driving. You said he deserved to go to Youth Authority for two years. And when he got out, you said he should be kicked off the island.''

Claire cringed under his attack. She drew in her legs and hunched over, avoiding his gaze. ''I know. I was wrong.''

Jake laughed out loud. ''That's what is so great about you, Claire. You can just instantly change what you believe so that no matter what, you're always somehow in the right. So long as you get what you want.''

"I've just learned a few things, Jake. Maybe I'm smarter than I was.''

"Very convenient.''

"So I'm a hypocrite. Call me what you want. I'm in love with you.''

Jake took a step back in surprise. "In love with me?'' He paused for a moment to compose his face into incredulity. "That's a nice touch.''

She met his eyes. "It's true.''

For a second he wavered. His expression softened. But then he steeled himself. "Even if it is, I don't care.''

"Yes, you do,'' Claire said.

"I don't need you to watch over me when I want to get drunk, Claire, and I don't need you covering for me when I don't do my homework. And I just plain don't need you,'' Jake said. He turned and walked away across the field.

"Yes, you do,'' Claire said again, this time to his retreating back.

Nina found the box in the storage room, a waterproof gray plastic tub with an airtight fitted top. She carried it up the stairs to her room and set it on the end of her bed.

She made sure her door was closed, then located a cigarette and popped it in the corner of her mouth. The top of the box came off easily and she peered down at the massive jumble of photographs.

These were all the shots that hadn't made it into one of the family's two big leather-bound photo albums. Those pictures had all been carefully chosen, but none showed what Nina wanted to see.

She took a big handful of photos and spread them out on her bed, some color, some very old grainy black-and-whites with scalloped edges. Some weren't photographs at all, really, but postcards from people she knew vaguely, from places she'd never been.

Most of the pictures were of people she did know. She found several of her mother and father at the Grand Canyon, so young they almost looked like a pair of very uncool teenagers. Nina sifted through the photos, making a small pile of pictures of her mother, ranging in age from childhood to just before she died. It was strange, but the more she looked at the pictures, the less they reminded her of her own faded memories of her mother, and the more they reminded her of ... someone else. Someone she couldn't quite place.

In pictures of her father alone, he always seemed very serious. In his army uniform, standing with his hands clasped behind his back, his creases like knife edges, his lieutenant's bars just so. Or in a business suit, or even later, wearing a white shirt and slacks, his casual look. It always looked like the photo was being taken against his will. Only when he was in a picture with Nina's mother did he smile and appear to be having fun. There was one shot in particular that caught Nina's eye, showing both her parents, separated by two little girls apparently punching each other out on the floor. Neither was looking down at the kids, but there was an expression between the two of them, both cocking their eyes at each other, identical looks of love mixed with amusement and maybe a little pride in the two brats at their feet.

Nina set that picture aside.

But she still hadn't seen what she was looking for. She dug out another pile, more shots of Claire, looking as solemn as their father, even as a tiny child—serious, thoughtful, aloof.

"Haven't changed, have you?" Nina said, smiling wryly at Claire. *Did you stand out in the yard staring up at the clouds even then? Did you manage to look down on everyone around you when you were just two feet tall? I'll bet you did.*

Then, from the pile in Nina's hand, one picture fell out. A skinny, gray-eyed girl with braces on her teeth, wearing a dress that revealed long, knobby legs, one with a Band-Aid on the knee. She was twisting a hank of hair around one finger. Nina turned the picture over. A note in ink said *Nina. 11th b'day.*

She leaned back on her pillows, holding the picture before her with both hands.

"So. This is what Benjamin thinks I look like." Nina smiled ruefully. "You ain't exactly Claudia Schiffer, kid," she told her image.

Eleventh birthday. Just two months before her mother died. Had her mother been there that day? Or had she been in the hospital? Nina couldn't remember.

She focused on the eyes in the picture. They were cocky, challenging eyes. "You think you own the planet, don't you?" she whispered.

If only that little girl had known what lay ahead. It would be only months until her mother died. Only a little while longer than that till she would be sent away to stay with her aunt and uncle.

For her own good.

"If only you knew, little Nina," she whispered.

She got up and walked over to the full-length mirror on the back of her closet door. She faced it and held the picture up beside her face.

Nina looked at her own present reflection and the small reflection of her past.

"You lost the braces," she said. "Filled out a little, which you never thought you'd do. The legs aren't quite as much like toothpicks, but now you have to shave them."

She realized the unlit cigarette was still dangling from her lips. "And you picked up one or two bad habits since then. Of course, you got rid of the Barbie dolls, so I guess it evens out."

She gazed into the eyes of five years ago. And back to the eyes in her mirror. Still challenging, still a little cocky, she noted, smiling wryly. She hadn't changed so much since then.

Then the smile faded and disappeared. "Only right now you look a little sad, Nina," she said.

She tucked the picture into her nightstand drawer. She would take it out and look at it the next time she had one of those dreams.

Nina

Here's the dream I call dream number two.

First of all, you have to get that dream feel, if you know what I mean. Where cause and effect aren't quite as clear as they are in real life. Where things can be sudden or very, very slow. Where you know things without knowing how you know.

It's always very gloomy in this dream. Like watching an old black-and-white movie on TV and turning the brightness knob way down. I see myself as if I'm some other person in the room. I see myself younger, at least

at first, and my mom is squat-
ting down, fussing with my
clothes, trying to straighten
this ridiculous bow on the
front of a ridiculous dress, wip-
ing my face clean, telling me to
smile and stand up straight.

And while she's doing this,
the little girl is tugging at her
clothes, undoing all the straight-
ening. She's playing with her hair,
leaving it tangled and wild. And
she's whining something about
not wanting to get all dressed
up. I don't want to, she says
in a little boohoo voice.

Then the little girl is older,
but still wearing the ridiculous

dress with the ridiculous bow. She's advancing uncertainly across a darkened room, toward a corner where all that she can see are two intense, staring eyes. She's afraid, but she can't stop because the eyes are telling her to come closer. Come here. Come here and give me some sugar.

And then, once more, the girl—the girl that is me—is somewhere else. She's lying in bed. And it's like maybe she's wet the bed because the sheets are warm and damp. She feels guilty; what if someone finds out? She plays with the ridiculous bow and pulls the covers over her head. The bow is magic. It can make her invisible.

And then I wake up. I feel guilty and ashamed. I also feel some lingering sense of undefinable pleasure, and that's the worst feeling of all.

And then the feelings fade. After a while I fall back to sleep and dream no more dreams.

Five

"Oh, no," Zoey said, pushing her way back through the crowd. "Oh, no. He's going to freak."

She backed away from the list that had been posted on the bulletin board near the principal's office. Other kids took her place, crowding in to read the names on the list. Zoey glanced apprehensively down the hallway, but in the early preclass crowd it was impossible to spot Lucas. The halls were jammed with loudly gossiping, shouting, teasing, worrying kids, grouped in twos and threes and fours around open lockers, milling in and out of rest rooms, jostling around the water fountain. The stairwells were slow-moving conveyor belts of humanity, going up and down, stopping, screaming, a moving picture painted with strokes of hair and patterned spandex, dull books and bright plastic, objects thrown and caught and dropped. The walls were hung with posters, exhortations to various teams taped to pale blue cinder-block walls.

From somewhere in the tight-packed mass Lucas emerged. Not the person Zoey wanted to see at that particular moment.

"Hey, Zo," he called. He grinned. "You're an island of calm beauty in a sea of noisy mediocrity."

She smiled uncertainly. "You're poetic this morning."

"Why wouldn't I be? I heard they're killing last period to hold an assembly. No French today. *Pas de français, chérie.*"

Zoey glanced nervously toward the list. "Uh-huh. Do you happen to know what the assembly is for?"

Lucas shrugged. "Probably the usual." He counted on his fingers. "It's either one, an anti-drug lecture, which I don't need, or two, an anti-booze lecture, which I also don't need, or three, an anti-sex lecture, which you give me every couple of days." He grinned to show he was just teasing. "Or else it's some student-government-pep-spirit-we're - better - than - everyone - else - so - let's - cheer-some-crowd-of-jock-dorks kind of thing."

"Partly it's a pep rally," Zoey agreed. "It's also to introduce the candidates for homecoming king and queen."

"That would fall into the category of cheering some crowd of dorks," Lucas said.

Zoey winced.

"Oh, hell, I'm sorry, Zoey," Lucas said quickly, coming to give her a hug. "Of course if you're up for it, that's totally different. You could never be a dork. I shouldn't have said that. There's nothing wrong with being more into the school thing than I am. I hope you win. Really. That is it, isn't it? I mean, you're one of the candidates, right?"

"Yes, actually I am," Zoey said. "But you know, it's not like people nominate themselves. And anyway, to be on the list you have to have received a dozen votes."

"See? At least a dozen people realize how great you are. Hell, I'm sorry I didn't think of it or I would have been the thirteenth."

"Lucas . . ."

"What?"

"I'm not the only one on that list."

"Well, sure, there are other aspiring homecoming queens."

"And kings."

"Now, I'm sorry, but those guys *are* dorks," Lucas said. "It's one thing for a girl. But a guy? Homecoming king? Why not just tattoo *dork* on your forehead and get it over with?"

"There are five guys on the list," Zoey said.

"Five poor dumb—"

"You're number three," Zoey said in a rush.

Lucas stared at her strangely. "No, I'm not."

"Yes, you are."

"Homecoming king. Me."

Zoey nodded.

"No."

"Yes."

"I'm going to kill Aisha. She did this. She was the one talking about what a great idea it would be. Where is she?" He spun around and searched the crowd.

"It took a dozen votes," Zoey pointed out.

"Twelve people said to themselves, Gee, I know, I'll nominate Lucas Cabral. He'd love it. Oh, yeah, Lucas has always wanted to be crowned King of the Dweebs, Lord of Losers."

"It's supposed to be an honor," Zoey told him.

"Not for *me*," Lucas cried. "I'm not one of *them*. I'm one of the outsiders, the rebels, the misfits. God, don't these people understand anything? You know what my old cellmates would say if they found out I was running for homecoming king? This is the kind of thing people like Jake do."

"He's on the list, too," Zoey said. "And why is it okay for me to do it, and that's cool, but it's totally different if it's you?"

Lucas looked confused. "Why is it different?" he repeated, playing for time.

"That's right, why is it different?"

"Um, because you're a girl?" he asked tentatively.

"Ha!" She pointed an accusing finger at him.

"Wrong answer. Um, look, I'm me and you're you. You are the type of person who should be homecoming queen. I'm the kind of person who should be homecoming barbarian."

The bell rang shrilly, blanking out the murmur of background noise. When it stopped, a collective groan went up from hundreds of mouths.

"I have to get to class," Zoey said frostily.

"Are you mad at me? You are, aren't you?"

"I'm not mad. I'm just a little hurt."

"Oh, that's worse," Lucas said.

"I'll try to get over it."

Lucas grabbed her hand as she started to walk away and pulled her to him. He tried to kiss her, but she was feeling resentful.

"Why should I kiss you?" she asked.

He shrugged. "Because you like it?"

Zoey gave him a dirty look. Then she kissed him lightly on the lips. "I'm still a little hurt," she said.

"Yeah, but *I* feel better!" he yelled after her.

"Go, Warriors, go, go. Go, Warriors, go!" Zoey shouted.

"Go, Warriors, go, go. Go, Warriors, go!" Aisha said a little less enthusiastically.

"Blah blahblah, blah blah. Blah blahblah, blah," Nina said.

Claire read a book.

"I knew he was going to do this," Zoey fumed. She half stood in the bleachers and searched the densely packed rows of kids. The pep rally was well under way in the big, aging, and somewhat aromatic gym, and Lucas was nowhere to be seen. "He's bailed, the coward. He's hoping they'll get him for skipping last period and make him ineligible."

"I wish I'd thought of skipping this whole thing," Nina said glumly. "Here we go again."

"We'll hit 'em again, we'll hit 'em again, we'll hit 'em one more time!" Zoey and Aisha cried on cue.

"We'll castrate them using blunt knives," Nina cried, causing several people nearby to turn and glare. "We'll gouge out their eyes and swallow them like oysters!"

Claire glanced up from her book, gave her sister a pained look, and shook her head slightly.

"Beat Camden, beat Camden, beat Camden," the chant began, becoming rhythmic and mesmerizing.

Nina jumped up, clenching her fists. "I vow total destruction on everyone from Camden. Kill the Camdenites! Slaughter them like pigs! They are the epitome of evil and must be wiped from the face of the earth! Forget football; we'll bomb the bastards! We'll make slaves of their children and whores of their women! Their men will be turned into beasts of burden!"

"Hi, Nina. That is you, isn't it?"

Zoey turned and saw her brother four rows back, looking amusedly in Nina's general direction. Nina seemed to blush.

"Hi, Benjamin!" Nina yelled up to him.

"I don't think you're taking this very seriously," Benjamin said in mock disapproval.

"I'm just trying to get into the whole fascist-barbarian-fundamentalist school-spirit thing," Nina explained.

A swell of noise blocked out Benjamin's next response. Zoey pulled Nina back down to her seat.

"Am I embarrassing you, Mom?" Nina asked Zoey.

"No, but they're getting to the nominations now," Zoey said, checking once more for any sign of Lucas. She bit her lip in vexation. The jerk.

Didn't it occur to him that at least a dozen people had shown some affection for him by voting for him? Didn't it occur to him that this was the student body's way of acknowledging that he wasn't the criminal creep they had thought he was?

"Lucas thinks I set this whole thing up, doesn't he?" Aisha asked.

"He'll get over it," Zoey grumbled.

"Make sure you tell him I didn't," Aisha said.

"I'll tell him, if I ever talk to the weasel again," Zoey said.

"Ah, true love," Nina remarked.

"With my luck Jake will win for king and I'll win for queen and then—" Zoey bit off the rest of her complaint as she saw Claire's head come up suddenly.

"Ooh, that got her attention," Nina said gleefully. "The king and queen do have to dance, right? Slow dance? And isn't there a big ceremonial kiss?"

"There is no ceremonial kiss," Claire said.

"Really?" Nina professed shock. "Then I guess the part where the royal couple retire to the couch in the teachers' lounge and try to make a little prince or princess . . . I guess that's not true, either."

Claire made her cool, superior smile. "The king and queen have an officially platonic relationship. You'd know all about that, wouldn't you, Nina? No kissing, no romance?"

Zoey and Aisha both swiveled their heads toward Nina, waiting for her next shot, but it didn't come. Instead Nina just made a face.

That was mean of Claire, Zoey thought. Nina's feelings had really been hurt. Although Nina had certainly been asking for it.

Nina yanked open her purse, pulled out a cigarette, and stuck it defiantly in the corner of her mouth.

"As you know, next week will be homecoming." Mr. Hardcastle had stepped up to the microphone. Cheers greeted his announcement. "And that means we have to choose a homecoming king and queen to officiate."

"Mr. Hardcastle for queen!" a voice yelled out.

"Good one," Nina said approvingly. "Wish I'd thought of it."

"We have a list of five candidates for each position . . ."

"He's not here," Zoey said. "He's not going to show up."

"As I read off the names, will the individuals please come down so we can all get a look at you . . ."

"Don't trip," Aisha whispered. "It makes a bad impression."

"Tad Crowley . . ."

"Isn't that the guy you made out with at that party?" Aisha asked. "You know, back when you and Jake were having a fight or something?"

"I didn't make out with him," Zoey said. "I just kissed him once."

". . . Louise Kronenberger."

"K-burger?" Nina said. "No way. You'll kick her butt, Zoey."

"The only votes she'll get are from guys she's slept with." Aisha smirked.

"So she'll be pretty big competition," Nina said.

". . . Jake McRoyan . . ."

Claire stood up and gave a completely uncharacteristic yell of support, joined by many others.

"Now I can die," Nina said, staring at her sister. "I've seen everything. The things people will do for romance."

"In your case, nothing," Claire shot back.

Jake was making his way, threading through the crowded stands to trot out onto the shiny gym floor and shake hands with Tad Crowley.

". . . Kay Appleton . . ."

"Oh, not her," Aisha said.

"You don't like Kay?" Zoey asked.

"She's such a phony. She always comes off like Miss Sweetness and Light. But she can turn instantly into this total barracuda."

". . . Lucas Cabral . . ."

Zoey stretched up to look. The only movement in the stands was Kay, making her way down to the floor.

". . . Lucas Cabral?" the principal repeated. "Is he out today? Well, we'll skip over him for now. On to our next candidate for queen . . . Zoey Passmore."

Zoey rose to her feet, still annoyed at Lucas but trying to force an appropriate smile.

"Zoey Passmore?" Aisha said in a disbelieving tone. "Who nominated her?"

"Really, she's such a witch," Nina said.

Six

Nina looked bleakly across the top deck of the ferry. As far as the passengers of her own age were concerned, it was divided up into impenetrable territories. In one zone Zoey and Lucas, arguing in Zoey's usual discreet, quiet, restrained way. Some distance away, in zone two, Aisha and Christopher were standing close to each other, murmuring and occasionally kissing.

Then, in zone three, there was Claire. Nina didn't have to make any special effort to avoid Claire. That was second nature to both of them.

Claire had begun by standing beside Jake at the forward rail, but Jake had pointedly moved away, taking a seat. Claire had pointedly followed him and now sat several feet from him on the same bench. They weren't speaking. Claire was reading and Jake was scowling, but it looked like a moral victory for Claire.

Only Benjamin sat alone. And only Nina stood alone.

Any other time, Nina would have felt no great hesitation about taking a seat beside him. They were friends, after all. But somehow the geography of the deck on this day would make it seem like she was being obvious. It was all boyfriends and girlfriends, even if Claire and Jake were in some type of limbo, and even if Zoey and Lucas were fighting.

Still, it was girls with the guys they liked. That was the arrangement, boyfriends and girlfriends, like it was in so much of life. And if she just went on over and plopped down beside Benjamin, wouldn't that make it look like she was trying to act like his girlfriend?

Claire had already teased her once about being in love with Benjamin. It had probably just been teasing. Certainly Claire couldn't know how true it was.

So it is true? Nina asked herself. Was it love she felt for Benjamin? Why should she? He obviously would never see her as anything but a friend.

She liked him, yes. But did she feel *that* way about him?

She stole a closer look at him, sitting there with earphones on, probably listening to some music she wouldn't even recognize, let alone enjoy. His eyes perpetually hidden behind the darkest-possible sunglasses.

She'd only seen his eyes a few times since he'd lost his sight. They were dark brown, and looked normal except that they never focused. They were always pointed just a little bit wrong. Benjamin could fake it better with his shades on. Then you didn't notice that no matter how hard he tried to look like he was gazing right into your eyes, he was really staring at nothing at all.

"Would I like you if you could see?" she whispered, unaware until she heard the words that she was speaking aloud.

She looked at his mouth. Did she want to kiss him?

Well, did she? That's what guys and girls did. It's what Lucas was doing to Zoey, trying to get her to lighten up. It's what Aisha and Christopher were doing.

She tried to picture it—Benjamin leaning close, his mouth moving toward hers.

The only time a guy had seriously tried to kiss her and touch her she had practically hurled.

Nina realized she was wringing her hands, twisting her fingers together. She put her hands at her sides and leaned back casually against the railing. She was fine. She was cool. Who cared what people thought of her, anyway?

Could you be in love with someone and *not* want them to at least kiss you? Was that possible? Because that was how she felt.

She could imagine telling Benjamin she loved him. She could even imagine him, somehow, feeling the same about her. But the thought of him looking at her with that look Nina had so often seen guys aim at her sister, at her best friend . . . That look made her sick. That was the truth: it just made her feel sick and brought memories flooding up out of the hidden parts of her mind. Of course, Benjamin couldn't look at her that way, or any way.

He couldn't stare at her. He couldn't even kiss her unless she wanted him to. And he couldn't touch her . . . He couldn't touch her unless she invited him to.

Zoey pouted, her chin raised loftily, gazing with feigned unconcern toward the island. If Lucas wanted to be a jerk, okay. He could be a jerk. If he wanted to act like he was too good to be involved in the lowly activities of the school, fine, then he was too good. She wasn't going to try to talk him into it anymore.

If he wanted to hurt the feelings of the people who had nominated him and basically slap them each in the face, it wasn't Zoey's problem.

Then she caught sight of Nina, standing alone by the railing. Maybe Nina's approach was better overall. Here Zoey was, unhappy because of a guy, and Claire was unhappy because of a guy. Aisha looked happy enough, but that was just one out of three, not very good odds.

Not that Nina seemed very happy at the moment, either. Something was bothering her. All day long she had been too shrill, too strange. Too *Nina*.

Lucas shifted on the bench beside her, drawing Zoey's attention back to him.

The jerk. What was worse was that he was acting like he just assumed he'd *win* homecoming king. Not exactly a sure thing when one of the other guys running was Jake. Jake had lots of friends in school. He was a very popular guy.

In fact, he was the best bet to win. Then, if Zoey

won herself, she would be in the awkward position of reigning with her former boyfriend.

She wondered how Lucas would feel about that.

A slow smile spread on Zoey's face. Had Lucas even thought of that possibility?

She sighed. "I've decided you're right, Lucas. If you don't want to be involved, I respect that."

"You do?" he asked suspiciously.

"Absolutely," she said. "It won't be so bad. First of all, I probably won't win. Second of all, even if I do, Jake will probably win for the guys and it will be like old times, me and him together. Me and Jake. Together."

Lucas looked at her impassively. "Nice try."

Aisha savored the feel of his lips on hers. Okay, she had been dumb to fight it so long. She was prepared to admit it, she had been dumb. She'd been attracted to Christopher right from the start, that was the truth. And she'd only resisted because she didn't want him to take her for granted. She'd wanted to make the point that they weren't doomed by fate to be together just because they were both black and living on a lily-white island in one of the country's whitest states. She had been standing up for the principle that fate didn't decide things, *she* decided things.

Big deal. Principle.

She smiled at him, and he smiled back. He murmured something sweet and she said something back.

Then they kissed again.

I wonder if he knows how I feel about him now? I wonder if he's smirking inside, thinking "I knew all along she couldn't resist me"? He's enough of an egomaniac to believe that.

Who cares? So he was right. Good for him. I'm glad.

Am I falling in love?

No. That's not what it is. It's too soon for that. Love takes forever to develop, as two people get to know each other and respect each other, share the same interests.

This is just . . .

He kissed her again.

. . . really nice.

She opened her eyes as they kissed and, to her surprise, realized his eyes were open, too. He was looking away.

She pulled back and turned to follow the direction of his gaze. There was Benjamin, sitting a distance away. And beyond him, an attractive woman who commuted on to Allworthy Island. She was twentysomething and had hiked up her skirt to be able to rub a sore foot.

Aisha cocked a dubious eyebrow at Christopher.

He looked back at her innocently. "I was wondering what Benjamin was listening to."

"You weren't looking at that woman?"

"What woman?"

Claire stared down at the pages of her book without reading any of the words. Her whole attention was on Jake, sitting a short distance away. He was staring out at the water, staring without moving or shifting his gaze, staring just so that he could avoid looking at her.

This was pathetic. She was making a fool of herself. In her entire life she had never thrown herself at any guy. She'd never had to; they had always thrown themselves at her.

Which was the way things ought to be.

Why was she doing this?

She stole a glance at Jake. Yes, yes, he was good-looking. But her boyfriends had always been good-looking. And she never would have acted this way over Lucas, back when she was going out with him, or over Benjamin, either.

Screw him. If he didn't want her anymore, to hell with him. She could take a hint. She'd never had to take a hint before, but she wasn't blind. Jake wasn't even being subtle. He'd told her to take a hike. Get lost.

No one had ever told her to get lost before. It was infuriating. The way it worked was that *she* dropped guys, not the other way around.

That's why she was so intent on getting Jake back, she told herself. She wasn't going to let him have the final word. No. She'd win him back and then *she* could dump *him*.

That was it. It was just a matter of pride. Pride mixed with a little guilt.

Either that or she really had fallen for him, really was in love the way she'd told him she was.

In which case, she was just being pathetic.

*　　*　　*

Nina was crammed onto the stairs that led down from the upper deck to the gangway, with Zoey and Lucas behind her and Benjamin behind them. Zoey and Lucas seemed to have reached a level of polite truce.

For some reason, the line wasn't moving. "Oh, man, don't hold me up at the end of a long day of school," Nina muttered.

"They're getting the living dead off first," Lucas said in a low voice. "There was a crowd of them below."

"Lucas, we call them elderly, not living dead," Zoey said.

"Whatever they are, they're pissing me off," Nina said.

"Why are you in such a hurry?" Zoey asked.

"Did someone die down there?" Aisha's voice filtered down from above.

"No, but someone's going to if I don't get off this stairwell!" Nina yelled. A businesswoman turned to look at her. "PMS," Nina explained.

"I thought you didn't believe in PMS as an excuse," Zoey said. "You never let me get away with it."

"I don't believe in it when it's you," Nina said. "Only when it's me."

"That sounds fair."

"Later I'm going to get a high-powered rifle, climb up on the roof, and shoot passersby while babbling about some conspiracy."

"Before you do that, do you think you can read to me for an hour or so?" Benjamin asked.

The line began to move down the stairs at last. "Sure, Benjamin," Nina said. "Just let me check in at home and change into something more comfortable than this full-length, diamond-studded, Naomi Judd dress I'm wearing." Nina looked down at her oversized shorts and baggy, layered top.

"Hey, don't try to fool me," Benjamin chided. "I know those aren't real diamonds."

Nina got off the boat and headed toward her house. Claire was heading to the same destination, of course, but half a block behind. It would never have occurred to either girl to walk together.

She stepped inside the large, well-decorated entryway and peeked to the right, into her father's dark, book-lined study. He wasn't there.

"Anyone home?" she yelled without much interest. There was no answer. It was Janelle's day off and her father would either have to wait for the next ferry home or catch the water taxi.

Nina slung her island bag with its load of books onto the antique oak dressing stand and headed straight down the hall to the kitchen. Lunch at school had involved dead cow, which she did not eat. So she was hungry now for some dead peanut.

She noticed the answering machine on the counter blinking twice. Two messages.

"Food first," she said. In the refrigerator she found raspberry preserves. With bread and peanut butter she made herself a sandwich and was just taking a first bite when she heard Claire come in the front door.

"Anyone home?" Claire asked.

"Me."

"Besides you."

"Just me and my sandwich," Nina said, taking a second bite.

"Have you checked the machine yet?"

"Go for it," Nina mumbled through a sticky lump of Jif.

Claire pushed the play button. What came on was the truncated, last few seconds of a machine-produced message.

". . . so we hope you will take advantage of this special opportunity to consider switching to AT&T. Don't forget: switching is free. Thank you."

After an electronic beep, the second message began.

"Hi, is anyone home? If anyone is home, please pick up. All right, I guess no one's home . . ."

"That would explain why we have the machine on," Nina muttered.

". . . Anyway, Burke, if this is your machine, this is Elizabeth calling. I just wanted to let you know that Mark and I will be coming in Sunday, probably late morning if the traffic isn't too bad. We look forward to seeing you and the girls. Bye-bye."

"Are you trying to mangle that sandwich?" Claire asked, staring at Nina disapprovingly.

Nina looked at the mess in her hand. She had crushed the sandwich, and now jelly and peanut butter were oozing through her fingers. She threw it into the trash and began washing her hands in the sink.

"Are you okay?" Claire asked.

"Fine," Nina said.

Claire sighed. "Great. Relatives. Well, there's no way to get out of it."

"Don't you like them?" Nina asked suddenly.

Claire shrugged. "They're relatives. Which means they think they have the right to ask me a lot of dumb, personal questions and tell a lot of boring stories."

"No, I mean, do you dislike them especially? Aunt Elizabeth and Uncle . . ."

". . . Mark." Claire supplied the name. "They've always seemed okay. I mean, Aunt E. is like Dad in a bad dress and with no sense of humor. And Uncle Mark is just boring. But at least they don't have kids."

"Why?" Nina asked while her mind whirled.

"Why what?"

"Why don't they have kids?" Nina pressed, as if it had become the most important question in the world.

"How would I know?" Claire said, giving her a frustrated look. "Maybe they don't like kids, or maybe one of them has some physical problem. Or maybe they're still waiting."

"They're too old."

"Aunt E.'s only forty, I think. It's still possible."

"I have to go," Nina said. "I have to read to Benjamin."

"Tell him hello," Claire said, sounding a tiny bit wistful.

"Yeah," Nina said. "I have to go right now." She ran from the house and didn't stop till she reached the circle. There she slumped against the cold marble war monument and labored to catch her breath. Her heart was pounding.

He was coming. She couldn't tell herself any longer that it had all been a false alarm.

She couldn't read to Benjamin, not now. He would know from her voice that something was wrong. He would ask her, or else he would tell Zoey to ask her, and Zoey would want to know.

But Zoey could never know. No one could.

He had told her that so many times, and she accepted it—no one would ever believe her.

Nina

Ah, yes, dream number three. Dream number three is one I've had several times. It's extremely embarrassing the way dreams are sometimes. Extremely strange. I guess all I can say is, hey, it's just a dream.

This dream starts out like two. My mom is dressing me in a cute little dress with a ridiculous bow on the front. Only this time I'm getting dressed for a party, a grown-up party; you know, where I'm the official cute kid. It's not much of a party from my point of view. It mostly involves staring up at massively tall adults, so tall that their heads aren't even clearly visible. They just seem to disappear in the mist.

Did I mention it's kind of foggy in this dream? It is. And dark again, like a grainy old picture. And all the adults are tall, like redwoods or something, going up and up until they seem to converge.

And I'm feeling weird, like I'm drunk. A drunk eleven-year-old in a bad dress. Everything kind of veering like the old Batman reruns, where things were always at an angle.

Anyway, in the dream I get

tired, so tired I almost can't
walk anymore. And then I see
the chair.

I climb up on the chair, which
is really tall, so tall it's like
climbing a mountain, only suddenly
there I am, sitting, and I'm
dangling my legs over the edge of
the seat, way above the
ground.

Which is when the embarrassing part comes in.

I suddenly realize all the tall
redwood people are staring at
me with these ax-murderer,
blood-hungry-vampire eyes. Staring and staring, and I squirm, being
understandably uneasy.

And then I realize I can feel the seat under my behind.

And then I realize I'm not wearing my dumb dress after all. I'm naked and starting to cry like a little baby.

And I never should have tried to go to the adult party, and I should have known better, and I knew I would be punished severely because it's my fault I'm there. My fault for being stupid.

When I wake up, I feel like throwing up.

And don't think I don't understand this dream, and the others, because I do. I know what it all means, although I

wish I didn't. I know the cause.
I know. I know the dreams and
the reality.

I just don't know how to
make either of them go away.

Seven

"It's new. It's called Polynesian Surprise," Nina said, dragging her fork through the slimy mess on her lunch tray the next day. "I think it involves pork. And either bean sprouts or white worms. I'm betting worms."

"Thanks for making me sick," Aisha said.

"Based on your vast and superior knowledge as seniors, are Polynesians more likely to cook with sprouts or worms?" Nina asked Zoey and Aisha.

"Why don't you just bring your lunch if you're going to complain about it every day?" Claire asked, taking the remaining vacant seat.

"Tradition," Nina said promptly. "I like complaining about the food." She managed a tight smile, though her sister's voice was like fingernails on a chalkboard to her.

"What is it with guys?" Zoey asked, suddenly changing the subject. "I mean, would it really kill Lucas to go along with this whole homecoming thing?"

"Why do you go out with guys if you're just

going to complain about them every day?" Nina asked, mimicking Claire.

"They're like food, my child," Aisha said in a low, husky voice, tossing her hair and closing her eyes to slits in a parody of worldly wisdom. "A necessary evil."

Claire shot Nina a mocking look. "Some people manage to do without. Sort of a starvation diet."

"And some people gorge on anything they can get," Nina shot back, more angrily than she'd intended.

"One point each," Aisha said. "A draw."

"I think all guys are at least partly jerks," Zoey said.

"Oh, it's worse than that," Aisha said. "All guys are *mostly* jerks."

"Trouble in paradise?" Nina asked Aisha, glad to divert attention from herself. Her leg was bouncing up and down under the table and she couldn't stop it. She felt wired and edgy. She hadn't slept well last night.

"No, not trouble," Aisha said. "Everything is great between Christopher and I."

"Me," Zoey said.

"Me what?" Aisha asked.

"Between Christopher and *me*."

"No way," Aisha argued.

"Yes. It's me."

"Who gives a rat's ass, Zoey?" Nina demanded. "Either way, things are fine, right?"

"Um, hi."

All four girls turned to look up at a tall, some-what frightened-looking guy.

"Hi, John," Zoey said.

"Um, hi, Zoey. Hi, Claire. Hi, Aisha." He winced and made a face, almost as if he were in pain. "Hi, Nina."

Nina made a mechanical half-smile. John Blount sat a desk away in her English class. "What's up, John? We were just this second having a fascinating discussion of grammar."

"Um . . . could I, uh . . . talk to you?"

"Sure, I still allow the little people to speak directly to me on occasion," Nina said.

"Like, over there?" John pointed.

Nina made a groaning noise deep in her throat. This had all the signs of something embarrassing. And this was not the day for it. "Nobody touch my Polynesian Surprise." She got up and followed John a few feet away, hoping against hope that he just wanted to borrow her homework or something.

"There's like a football game tonight," John said, digging his hands deep into his pockets.

"Thank you for letting me in on that, John."

He laughed, then blushed. "Do you want to, like, go with me?"

Nina cringed, for herself and for him. She hated saying no, not that it came up all that often. "Actually, um, John, I wasn't going to go to the game."

"That's all right," he said quickly. "We could do something else."

"It's nice of you to offer, but I don't think so,"

91

Nina said, beginning to feel the electric edge of panic.

"Oh."

"Look, it was sweet of you to ask, all right?"

"So you're saying you don't want to go out with me?"

"I guess that sums it up," Nina said.

John's face instantly turned angry. "You think because your dad is rich I'm not cool enough for you?" he demanded, his voice rising. "Or is it because Zoey's your *real* boyfriend?"

He turned and walked away. Nina watched him go for a second, extremely reluctant to have to face her friends, who had, without any doubt, heard John's parting shot.

She drew a deep, steadying breath and turned back to them, sliding heavily into her seat. She covered her eyes with one hand. "What was it we were saying about guys being jerks?"

"I used to think he was a nice guy," Zoey said angrily.

"He is a nice guy," Nina said flatly. The edginess and panic were gone now, replaced by disgust for the way she had handled things. "He just thought I was trying to embarrass him, I guess."

"Hey, if he wants to ask you out, he's got to accept the possibility the answer will be no," Aisha said.

"Or the absolute certainty," Claire said.

Nina dug her fork viciously into the Polynesian Surprise. "Look, can we just drop it? John's cool; it was my fault."

"It was not your fault," Aisha said, outraged. "Tell her, Zoey."

"He had no right to dump on you," Zoey agreed.

"I could have said yes and then he wouldn't have said that, all right? So it's my fault, too," Nina said. She twisted the fork and bit her lip. She felt like pounding something. Screw the principal— she wanted a cigarette. She began digging in her purse.

"I can't believe I'm hearing this prefeminist *blame the woman* b.s. from you, Nina," Aisha said. "What are you going to tell me next? That it was your fault because you lured him on with your short skirt?"

"I'm not wearing a skirt," Nina muttered, still looking for her cigarettes.

"That's just an example of the kind of crap you're saying," Aisha ranted, waving her hand dismissively. "Hamster Boy there had no reason to say that. Or drag Zoey into it."

"Sorry," Nina told Zoey.

"You're hopeless," Aisha said. "She's hopeless. It's a good thing you *don't* date, Nina. I mean, God, you'd be thinking it was your fault if you didn't want to do the old in-out on the first date. You have the right to say no without some guy calling you names."

"Damn it, can we just drop this!" Nina's sudden explosion silenced everyone within twenty feet.

"Get a grip, Nina," Claire said quietly.

Nina was on her feet. Her chair fell over backward, clattering noisily. "*You* get a damned grip, Claire. It's nobody's business, all right? I don't tell any of you what to do, so just leave me alone. It's not . . . It's my problem. Okay?"

"Okay, Nina," Zoey said, in the kind of cautious voice people use to talk to lunatics and vicious dogs. "Come on, we didn't mean to upset you."

"I'm not upset," Nina said, suddenly feeling empty and deflated. "I'm . . ." She raised her hands helplessly. "I'll see you guys on the ferry."

She turned and walked away, fighting the tears until she could find some private place to let them fall.

Eight

Claire had brought a change of clothing to wear to the football game that night. Extracurricular activities were always difficult for island kids, given the inflexible ferry schedule. Games started at six thirty, which meant she would have had to take the four o'clock home, arriving at four twenty-five, run to her house, shower, change, then run back and catch the five ten returning to the mainland. Rather than getting forty-five rushed minutes on the island, she usually brought extra clothes over with her for dates and games and changed in the girls' locker room.

When she entered the locker room, she heard laughing voices—Zoey and Aisha, also changing. Zoey was drying her hair and yelling over the noise.

"You mean Jake told her to go away?" Zoey said. "You actually heard this?"

"Cross my heart!" Aisha yelled back. "At practice on Wednesday."

Claire faded behind a bank of lockers and waited.

Zoey turned off the hair dryer. "Excuse me? *Wednesday?* And you're telling me on Friday? Friday afternoon? Sometimes I despair for you, Eesh. You'll never make a great gossip. Nina would have told me within eight seconds."

"It didn't occur to me. I do have my own life to lead."

"And she's still going after him," Zoey said, marveling. "That has to be a first for Claire. Normally, all she has to do with a guy is look at him and he's ready to rip zipper."

"Well, I haven't known her as long as you have."

"Take my word for it. When she was in sixth grade, she had tenth-grade guys after her."

"Huh. Let me smell that perfume. I don't see why guys would be all that crazy over her. That's nice. Let me use some."

"Hmm, let's see. She has a perfect body, great hair, a beautiful face. She's very smart and manages to have that whole air-of-mystery thing going—you know, dark, mysterious eyes, the way she walks and all."

"Plus, she's kind of a bitch," Aisha added with a laugh. "Christopher says that's why he likes me."

"She's not really," Zoey said, sounding thoughtful. "Claire just lives in her own world. She's very . . . I don't know the right word—"

"Superior? Arrogant? Snotty? Condescending? Don't do your eyebrows that way. Watch me—like this, it's easier."

Claire smiled wryly. It was always useful to hear how other people saw you.

". . . ow, damn, that hurt."

"But it works better," Aisha said.

Claire crept back to the locker room door. She opened it noisily and let it slam shut. Instantly Zoey and Aisha fell silent.

"Hi," Claire said.

"Claire," Aisha said, "we were just talking about you."

"Good things, I hope," Claire said mildly.

"Why, are there *bad* things?"

"Have you seen Nina?" Zoey asked Claire.

"She went back home," Claire said.

"Huh," Zoey said. "I thought she was thinking of coming to the game for a change."

Claire raised an eyebrow. "After that scene at lunch, I don't think so."

"That shouldn't upset her," Zoey said unconvincingly. "No one noticed. Besides, people expect Nina to do surprising things. She shouldn't be embarrassed."

"Yes, she should," Claire said. "Not that I want to be snotty or condescending, but I think she needs to learn to deal with members of the opposite sex."

She was pleased to see Aisha and Zoey exchange an uneasy look.

"Maybe she doesn't like guys," Aisha suggested.

"Eesh!" Zoey chided.

"Look, it wouldn't bother me," Aisha said.

"I'm open-minded. I'm just saying maybe Nina's gay."

"She's not gay," Claire said. "She's just weird."

"Are you sure?" Aisha pressed. "You two aren't the closest sisters on earth. Maybe it's possible she's keeping it a secret from you, too."

"I know plenty of other girls who don't date," Zoey said.

"Don't get defensive, Zo," Aisha said, laughing. "Even if she is a lesbian, it doesn't mean she has the hots for you. Although . . . you two are pretty close."

"You know, you sound like a guy, Aisha," Claire said. "Every time you tell a guy no—no to anything—the first brilliant theory they come up with is that you're gay. It never, ever occurs to the guy that maybe he's just a toad."

"Not every guy is a toad," Aisha said. "But Nina always says no. Has she ever had a relationship that lasted more than one date? Has she ever mentioned being interested in a guy?"

"Look, Nina's just Nina, all right?" Zoey said hotly. "She has the right to be however she wants."

"She's not gay," Claire said. "So you two can rest easy. I think there is a guy she's interested in."

Claire was gratified by the way both Zoey and Aisha stared at her, jaws open.

"Who?" Aisha asked.

"She would have told me," Zoey said.

Claire smiled. "Look, I've told you all I can

98

without indulging in gossip. You wouldn't want me to gossip about my own sister behind her back, would you?''

"Why doesn't she go out with this guy, then?" Aisha asked.

Claire shrugged. "It's all one-way. I don't think he even knows she's alive."

"Poor Nina," Zoey said thoughtfully.

"Oh, well," Claire said lightly. "I guess unrequited love happens to everyone sooner or later." She turned on the water and began splashing her face. "Even to girls with perfect bodies and that whole air-of-mystery thing."

"Of course she heard us talking about her; she was toying with us," Aisha grumbled. "You think *air of mystery* is just a phrase that happened to pop into her mind? Now she thinks I think she's arrogant."

"She thinks I think she's very smart and has a perfect body. She'll think I'm jealous of her," Zoey complained.

They emerged from the gym, and Aisha glanced at her watch. "We have time to kill. You want to go downtown?"

"We could get my folks' real car and drive out to the mall," Zoey suggested.

"Do you have the keys?"

"Sure. I can take the car anytime, as long as I'm sure my parents are staying on the island. I'll give my mom a quick call, then we hit the garage and get in a couple hours of shoppage."

Fifteen minutes later they were on the road toward the mall. "Do you think Claire was telling the truth about Nina?" Aisha asked. She didn't want to press the issue too much because she knew Zoey was sensitive about it.

"Who knows with Claire?" Zoey said.

"Nina would have told you if she was hot for some guy," Aisha said.

"Nina can't keep secrets," Zoey agreed. "But by the same token, she could never keep secret about being gay if she were. Personally, I think Nina's just . . . original."

Aisha nodded, unconvinced, as they cruised the mall parking lot.

"Is that a space?" Zoey asked.

"No, handicapped."

"How about—"

"Motorcycle."

"There," Zoey said, quickly pulling into an open space. "Hey, isn't that Christopher?"

Aisha followed the direction Zoey was pointing. Just visible through several parked cars was Christopher, passing out of sight. Aisha opened the door quickly and stood up, ready to yell to him. But then she stopped herself.

Zoey climbed out, too. "There he is," she said, "see?"

"Yes, I see," Aisha said. She met Zoey's puzzled stare. "I also see that girl he's following." She had a blond ponytail that fell straight down her back to the middle of a behind that hung half out of a pair of Daisy Dukes.

"They're just walking in the same direction," Zoey said.

"And now?" Christopher had drawn even with the girl and was smiling. The girl smiled back and said something that made Christopher laugh.

"Now he's just saying hi," Zoey said.

"Uh-huh. Come on. But let's stay back."

"You want to follow him?" Zoey sounded shocked. "You want to spy on him?"

"No way. But we did come here to go to the mall, and if we just happen to all be walking in the same direction—"

"So we're not spying?"

"No."

"But we should be careful not to let him see us?" Zoey asked.

"You're very quick, Zoey, anyone ever tell you that?" Aisha set off, edging along the lines of parked cars, watching as Christopher opened the glass door of the mall entrance and held it open for the girl.

Christopher and the girl disappeared from view inside. Aisha, with Zoey alongside, entered a minute behind him. Christopher and the girl were standing just a few dozen paces inside. Aisha grabbed Zoey's arm and pulled her behind a pod of telephones.

She peeked cautiously around the side. The quality of Christopher's smile had changed, becoming subtler. Worse yet, the girl was playing with her hair, pulling the ludicrously long ponytail forward as if displaying it for Christopher.

Aisha slid back behind the phones. "Did you see that?" she asked Zoey.

"I wasn't looking," Zoey whispered.

"She's playing with her hair and smiling," Aisha said.

Zoey winced. "That scrote."

Zoey peeked cautiously around the side. "She's gone now," she whispered. "Christopher's over at the ATM getting some money out."

"You're sure she's gone?" Aisha asked.

"I didn't see her."

"Check again," Aisha said.

"Okay." Zoey leaned out again. "Now they're both gone."

"He's probably gone after her," Aisha said bitterly.

"I'm sure it wasn't anything. Maybe he knows her from somewhere. Besides, she left first, right? So it couldn't have been anything."

Aisha narrowed her eyes. "Uh-huh."

"Look, Eesh, you can't get jealous every time Christopher talks to a member of the opposite sex."

"They were grinning like baboons and she was playing with her hair," Aisha snapped. "I'm not blind."

"Maybe she just has a habit of playing with her hair."

"And maybe *he* just has a habit of trying to pick up on girls at the mall." She bit her lip, trying without much success to relax and stop the spiral of irrational anger that was building inside her.

"Did you guys ever say it was supposed to be a steady thing?" Zoey asked.

The question took Aisha by surprise. "We never said much of anything," she admitted. "But, I mean, I assumed . . ."

"Talk to him about it at the game tonight," Zoey suggested. "Straighten it out. Maybe all he needs is for you ask him flat out whether you guys are going to make it monogamous. Talk before you get all upset, okay?"

"I'll talk," Aisha said, "but I'll go ahead and start getting upset just in case."

Nine

Claire finished getting dressed for the evening, emerged from the gym, and walked toward Portside Weymouth, wandering through the quaint shops that were so much like a somewhat larger, better-stocked version of North Harbor. She bought a pair of silver earrings at one shop and almost bought a sweater at another before deciding against it. Then, glancing at her watch, she decided to find something to eat. It was either eat now or wait and be forced to consume the hot dogs the team booster club sold at the game.

She walked through the cool, busy, cobble-stoned streets and aimed for Big Mikey's, a slightly disreputable but cheap diner that was an after-school hangout for Weymouth High kids.

Big Mikey himself was behind the counter, looking dissatisfied and a little dangerous. Claire sat down at an empty stool at the neon-trimmed counter. "Hi, Big."

"Ah, the banker's daughter," he replied, managing a half-smile. "What'll you have?"

"Foie gras?"

"Sorry. Just ran out of foie gras."

"Okay, then I'll have a chicken breast sandwich and a salad," Claire said.

"Uh-huh," Big Mikey muttered. He glanced meaningfully toward the corner of the room.

Claire looked toward the corner but saw nothing of any particular interest.

"In the last booth," he said out of the corner of his mouth.

Claire looked again. From her angle, she couldn't see a thing. She held up her hands help-lessly. "What? Is there something I'm supposed to be seeing?"

"Jake and some other kid."

Claire was surprised—both that Jake was there and that someone like Big Mikey would know that she cared. "So what?" she asked, acting noncha-lant.

"The two of them ordered tall Cokes. Which they've been drinking for an hour now."

"So what, she repeated," Claire said impa-tiently.

"So the Cokes never get empty, but a little paper bag keeps appearing from under the table."

It took Claire a moment to figure out what the man was telling her. When she understood, she was shocked. "Are you telling me Jake's drinking? He has a game tonight."

"Yeah, and I have a twenty-dollar bet I'm going to lose if the star running back is faced on cheap rum. And it is cheap rum; I can smell it from here. Not to mention that my business could be pretty

well screwed if some cop wanders in here and decides I'm letting underage kids drink.''

Claire cursed under her breath.

"Exactly,'' Big Mikey agreed. He shook his head. "You'd think after what happened to his brother . . .'' He let his words trail off, looking down in embarrassment. "Sorry. I wasn't thinking.''

"Neither is he,'' Claire said. "Damn. You want me to get him out of here, I guess?''

"I was just getting ready to do it myself,'' Big Mikey said. "But I think it might go a little more peacefully if you do it.''

Claire cursed again, this time silently. Damn it, what did Jake think he was doing, getting drunk a few hours before the game? Come to think of it, what did he think he was doing getting drunk, period?

She drew in several deep, steadying breaths.

"I'll buy your dinner if you can do it without any dishes getting broken.''

Claire climbed off the stool and walked over to the booth. The second guy was Dave Voorhies. He and Jake were hunched morosely over two Cokes that were suspiciously light in color. "Hi, Jake. Dave.''

Jake looked up quickly. His eyes were a little blurred, but he focused. Good, he probably wasn't too far gone.

"Well, damn, if it isn't Killer Claire,'' Jake said in a rowdy voice.

Claire forced herself not to react. It wouldn't

help things for her to get emotional. "Jake, I was thinking maybe it might be time to head up to the school. You know, the game tonight?"

"I know the game, Claire, Claire, Killer Claire."

His voice was slurred. He might be drunker than she had realized. She forced a cool smile. "You know, you're supposed to be *in* the game."

Jake slapped his forehead in mock surprise. "No!"

"Yes," Claire countered.

"You know," Jake said, leaning forward to stare at Dave, "I really, really liked her, you know?"

"I can understand that," Dave said with a leer in her direction.

"Don't do that," Jake said sharply.

"I didn't do nothing."

"I saw that look," Jake said. "I was telling you something. See"—he grabbed Dave's arm—"she . . . see, I really liked her, only, you know what she did? And then, how can I?" He sat back. "How?"

He is drunk, Claire realized. Major drunk. Two hours before game time. "Jake, stop being a hole. You could get kicked off the team if you show up drunk for a game."

He looked up at her with moist, defiant eyes. But she could see the light of reason beginning to dawn just a little. "I'm not drunk."

"Sure you are, dude," Dave pointed out helpfully. "We're both drunk."

"I am?" Jake acted as if it was a pleasantly surprising bit of news.

"Your coach will dump you," Claire said.

107

"This is your senior year; you don't want to get dropped from the team."

"What the hell do you care?"

Claire sighed. "I care, okay?"

"You don't give a damn about me," Jake said flatly. "You just feel guilty."

"You're wrong, Jake," Claire said in a steady voice, trying to shut out Dave's blinking, unfocused stare. "I do care. I'm here trying to help you because I care. If you don't want to believe that, fine. But what I want to do right now is get you sobered up and ready for the game."

He shook his head sadly. Then he lifted his head and stared at her. "You are very, very, very beautiful."

"So I've heard," Claire said dryly.

"I have to go and get ready for the game," Jake said with sudden, drunken decisiveness.

"Let's go." Claire took his arm and guided him up out of the booth. He wavered and almost sat back down. But at last he was standing, weaving back and forth a little.

"Hot shower, then cold shower," Big Mikey said, still behind the counter. "And fill him with fluids; that will help him to get rid of the alcohol and keep from dehydrating."

"Come on, Jake," Claire said, leading him toward the door. "That's it. Yes, it's best if you put one foot in front of the other."

Claire walked Jake up the hill to the school. The sun was just beginning to turn the sky pink in the west, throwing the Gothic-looking brick face of the school building into ominous shadow.

He walked sullenly beside her, wavering a little less, sweating profusely as the alcohol worked its way through his system. Just by the side of the building he tore free and made a dash for the bushes. Claire looked away and tried not to hear the disgusting retching sounds that seemed to go on and on.

At last he emerged, pale and shaken. "Must have been something I ate," he said weakly.

"Yeah," Claire said. She took his arm again and propelled him toward the gym, taking the back way to avoid any kids who might be hanging around out front. Only a small, startled-looking group of juniors was in the back, passing a joint among themselves. Claire ignored them, and she and Jake reached the rear doors of the gym.

"Girls' shower," Claire said. "Some of your team might already be in the boys' shower. Girls' locker room will be empty."

"Too bad," Jake joked feebly.

They skulked around the edge of the bright basketball floor and entered the girls' locker room. The only girls who tended to use the showers after-hours were island kids and, as Claire knew, they were all accounted for. The lights were off, so she turned them on, reassured that the room was in fact empty.

Claire guided Jake to the shower, turned the water on full and hot, and tested it. "Get undressed and get under."

Jake gave her a bleary rendition of a rakish look. "Are you trying to take advantage of me?"

"Jake, right now you are a thoroughly disgusting creature," Claire said. "You're sweating like a pig and you reek of vomit. Just get undressed and get under the shower." She turned away and went to her locker. She dug out a towel and a bar of soap and set them on the bench. Then she pulled out a small blue bottle of Listerine.

She crossed over to Zoey's locker. Out of the corner of her eye she caught a glimpse of Jake under the shower. She fought down the impulse to satisfy her curiosity and concentrated on remembering Zoey's birthday instead. She tried the numbers out on the combination lock, and it opened easily. In Zoey's locker she rummaged until she found a tiny bottle of Murine and the vitamins Zoey popped every day before gym class. She dumped two of these and the Murine on her towel.

"Jake, I'm going to bring you some stuff," Claire warned. "Turn away."

He gave no sign of having heard her, but as she approached he was leaning headfirst against the tile wall, looking like he might fall over. "Here," she said, keeping her eyes fixed on his. "Take these with some shower water."

He held out a hand and swallowed the vitamins obediently.

"Soap. It's Camay. Sorry, I don't have anything more manly. There's a towel and some mouthwash and some Murine over by the sinks. Drink all the water you can hold. I'll wait outside and make sure no one else comes in.''

Jake nodded mutely.

Claire turned and walked outside into the gym. She leaned against the wall and realized she was perspiring herself. She let out a long, shaky sigh.

Well, at least she hadn't stared or broken out in giggles. All in all, she had handled her first close encounter with a completely naked guy pretty well. Like a professional nurse.

Although certain images were now pretty well burned on her brain.

After fifteen minutes, the locker room door opened. Jake came out, dressed again in his same clothes, looking pale but alive. His eyes were downcast.

''Did you drink plenty of water?'' Claire asked him.

''Gallons.''

''Good. Alcohol dehydrates your body.''

''What time is it?'' he asked.

''It's five fifteen.''

''I have to suit up in forty-five minutes,'' he said anxiously.

''You should eat if you think you can keep it down,'' Claire said.

Jake nodded passively.

''Probably not Big Mikey's,'' Claire said. ''Come on.''

They walked a few blocks in silence, ending up at a little diner, where Claire ordered Jake poached eggs, toast, large quantities of juice and coffee, and an Alka-Seltzer to help him keep it all down. As he ate, he seemed to revive. Color came back to his cheeks. His movements became more crisp and efficient. His eyes focused clearly.

"You want anything else?" Claire asked.

He shook his head. "I think I can make it now. I'm still woozy and I won't be a hundred percent, but I won't fall on my face. At least I don't think I will."

"I thought falling on your face was the whole point of football."

Jake didn't smile. Instead he looked down at his coffee. "Coach would have cut me if I'd shown up like I was," he said. "I . . . I have to say thanks. I mean, thanks. Thanks."

"No problem," Claire said, feeling a sudden welling of emotion.

"I, uh . . . Look, I don't know what's going to happen with us, all right? But anyway, you saved my ass."

Claire allowed herself an impish smile. "It is a really nice ass."

Jake groaned, but with some of his old good nature. "Please don't remind me. Ever."

"Jake." She paused. "Jake, why were you drinking?"

He shrugged. "Dave had a bottle."

"You didn't used to drink," Claire said, as gently as she could.

"It's been a bad week. It's been a bad couple of weeks."

Claire reached across the table and took his

hand. He gave her fingers a light squeeze, then bit his lip as if he regretted it. "I have to go," he said. "I need major warm-up. I have to try and sweat out the rest of this stuff."

"I'll see you at the game," Claire said.

"I'll be the one falling on my face." He stood up and dug crumpled dollars out of his jeans to pay the check.

"I'll be the one cheering while you do," Claire said.

Ten

"Here he comes," Aisha muttered out of the side of her mouth.

Zoey was next to her in the crowded, rowdy bleachers with Lucas. Twilight had followed sunset, and the stadium lights bathed the field in unreal, bluish brilliance, turning red uniforms black and casting impenetrable shadows that completely concealed the faces of the players within their helmets.

"I don't see him!" Zoey yelled over a sudden roar of excitement. "Oh, wait, now I see him. He's looking for you."

"Are you sure about that?" Aisha asked. She plastered a phony smile of welcome on her face and waved her hand back and forth. "Christopher! Here he comes, the snake."

"Give him a chance," Zoey advised.

"Is something going on?" Lucas asked.

"No," Zoey said. "Nothing that would interest someone like yourself who is so far above all this day-to-day school stuff that occupies smaller minds like mine and Aisha's."

Lucas sighed, shook his head glumly, and returned his attention to the game.

Christopher came winding his way through the seated kids and parents and townspeople, all either talking, cheering, or eating. He gave Aisha a big smile. She searched it for signs of falseness.

"Hi, Christopher," Zoey said.

"Hey," Lucas said, lifting one hand in a sort of greeting.

Christopher gave Aisha a quick kiss. "What's the score?" he asked Lucas.

"Nothing to nothing," Lucas said. "But our nothing looks a little better."

Aisha scooted over to make room for Christopher beside her. "So, what have you been doing all afternoon?" she asked brightly.

Christopher shrugged. "Stuff. Picked up my paycheck for the paper deliveries. I'm rich enough to buy you a dog, if you want. You can even get chili."

"No thanks," Aisha said. "Did you do anything after you picked up your check?"

"Yes, yes, no, no, no, look out!" Christopher yelled. Down on the field, Jake got the ball and ran five yards before being tackled.

"That had to hurt," Lucas said sympathetically.

"So you just picked up your check," Aisha persisted.

"Hm-hm. Bought some socks. That was pretty much the high point."

"Really? Socks?" Aisha asked, sounding terribly interested.

"They're going to the blitz," Christopher said.

"Uh," Lucas agreed.

"So where did you buy these socks?" Aisha asked.

A roar from the Camden fans across the field elicited a response from the local faithful.

"What?" Christopher shouted.

"I said, where did you buy the damned socks!" Aisha yelled.

Christopher looked at her skeptically. "Why?"

"Because I'm just curious. Zoey and I are both curious about where you bought your socks because we both would like to know where a good sock store is," Aisha said.

"Yeah," Zoey agreed unconvincingly. "Socks. We love socks. I probably have, oh, twenty pairs. All different colors and stuff."

"I bought them at that place downtown. You know, that place with the neon sign in the window shaped like a wave?"

"Spinners?" Aisha asked, beginning to seethe.

"Yeah, that's it."

"You should have tried the mall," Aisha said. "They have lots of great sock stores there. Cheaper than Spinners."

Christopher shrugged. "The mall's miles out there. I didn't want to go all that way just to save fifty cents on a pair of socks."

There it was, Aisha realized. He had lied. A flat-out lie. She felt Zoey's hand surreptitiously squeeze her arm in solidarity.

She had seen him coming on to another girl. And

116

then he had lied about it. Which meant there could have been lots of other flirtations with lots of other girls. And he was probably prepared to lie about them, too.

Or maybe it was nothing. Maybe he knew the girl from somewhere and was just saying hi. Maybe he forgot he was at the mall.

That's right, Aisha, she thought, *you can come up with some kind of bogus explanation if you try hard enough.*

"So, what did *you* do today?" Christopher asked her. "I hope it was something as exciting as buying socks."

"No," Aisha muttered. "I guess you had more fun than I did."

On the field Jake caught the ball and ran for a touchdown. The Weymouth High fans went nuts. Aisha was the only one left sitting. She sat through the next two quarters, but at the half, with Weymouth High well in the lead, they all headed for rest rooms and the munchie stands.

Zoey and Lucas peeled off, still sniping at each other about homecoming royalty. Christopher took Aisha's hand and drew her under the darkened seats. Overhead there was the clatter of footsteps on the boards.

"I haven't had a chance to kiss you all day," he said, taking her in his arms.

She forced a smile. "And you were thinking about me all day?"

"Every minute," he said. "Every second."

"I'm sure there were a few minutes here and

there when you might have thought about something else."

He held up his hand as if taking an oath. "On my Boy Scout honor."

"Were you a Boy Scout?"

"Nope." He grinned and lowered his mouth toward hers. She gave him a grudging kiss.

It would have been easy to make him admit the truth. She and Zoey had both seen him. And the fact that he lied about being in the mall just proved that he was hiding something. The girl with the long blond ponytail? Some other girl he had met later? She could drag the truth out of him right now. Was he seeing other girls? Was he going to go on seeing other girls?

"We can do better than that," he said in a lower voice. He tilted back her head with his hand, and she let him. He pressed his lips to hers, and she let him. And when he opened his mouth, so did she.

She could force the truth from him. But what if she didn't like the answer? What if for him she was just one among many? How could she stand hearing that, when for her he had so quickly become the only one?

The front of the Geiger home had a balcony. The door to the balcony was halfway between Nina's room and the room her uncle would soon be staying in. Nina seldom went out on the balcony. Even just two stories up, it excited her fear of heights. But she went out on it now, keeping a nervous eye on the white-painted crosshatched railing. By looking west, she could see the water through the trees in the front yard, and beyond the water, the lights of Weymouth. A brilliant white point, like a star fallen to earth, marked the school's stadium where Zoey and Claire and Aisha would be.

She walked to the end of the balcony nearest her own bedroom and pressed up against the railing there to check if she could see inside her bedroom.

The view was clear. She could see most of her bed, the far closet door, her dresser. She went back into the house and lowered the blinds in her room. Then she went back out onto the balcony and checked. This time nothing was visible but the tiniest sliver of escaping light. At least that worked. With her blinds drawn, she would be able to hide.

She got off the balcony and closed the door behind her. Then she went to her bed and spilled out the contents of an Ace Hardware bag. She had a brass sliding lock with screws in a shrink-wrapped plastic card and a Phillips screwdriver. She carefully read the directions on the back of the lock, then tore it open. The screws spilled out and she had to hunt for them through the folds of her quilt.

Once they were gathered up, she went to her door again and knelt to get a close look at the painted wood molding. She placed the lock where she thought it should go, and with her other hand tried to place the little eye. The two halves of the lock didn't match up. At least not perfectly.

Nina stared at the door in frustration. The problem seemed to be that the molding stuck out from the door. She placed the main part of the lock against the door this time and the eye against the molding. Still no good. She would have to damage the molding.

Too bad she'd never taken any shop classes. The use of tools wasn't her strong point.

She trotted downstairs to the kitchen and dug in the kitchen drawer for something useful. Then her gaze settled on a knife. It was a very sharp, serrated knife with a short blade, no more than three inches long. She stuck this carefully in her back pocket and ran back upstairs.

She went at the molding, using the serrated knife to chop and gouge out a section long enough for the eye and deep enough to lie flush with the door. It took nearly twenty minutes before she had the lock in place, screwed down with its brass screws.

She closed the door and tried the lock several times. It stuck a little, but with some effort she could slide the bolt into the eye and make it work.

It wouldn't stop someone determined to get in. But it would slow someone down and force them to make noise. She nodded in grim satisfaction. He wouldn't want to make noise, not here in *her* house.

Nina scooped up the splinters and sawdust she'd generated and dropped them in the trash. Then she picked up the knife, intending to take it downstairs.

But with the black plastic handle in her palm, she hesitated. With unwilling eyes she stared down at its wicked blade. Would she ever use it? Would she ever really use it?

Would she have used it before, years ago, if she'd thought of it then?

Probably not. She wasn't that kind of person.

She sat down on the edge of her bed, still holding the knife. She pulled open her nightstand drawer and took out the picture of herself back then. A part of her mind told her that she wasn't acting rationally, that this was all unnecessary. No one would be stupid enough to try to . . . to reach her here, in her own house, with her father asleep just down the hall.

Nina laughed, a short, bitter sound as she looked at the picture of a more innocent, unafraid girl. It wasn't about being rational anymore. Reason had been lost forever, after that first time. "You were so dumb, you didn't even know what was going on," she told the photograph.

The first time had been so innocent. Just a request to sit on her uncle's lap in the family room of his house. And then, just innocent questions. Did she like Uncle Mark? Of course, she'd replied. Did she like him a lot? Sure, she liked him. That was good, because her uncle really liked her, too.

He thought she was a very pretty young lady. Someday the boys would go crazy for her, someday they would be all over her. No, not likely, she'd answered. Why not? She'd shrugged.

Claire was prettier, Nina had told him.

Yes, he'd said, but Claire wasn't as nice as Nina. Nina was nice, wasn't she? She wanted to be nice to people who cared about her and thought she was pretty. Didn't she?

That's good, he'd said. Give your uncle a little kiss. You can do better than that. Give your uncle a real kiss. Like this. Did she like that? Did she?

Nina realized her hands were shaking. She had dropped the knife on the floor.

Yes, she had answered, tucking down her chin and feeling almost sick.

Did she like that?

Yes. She'd said yes. And from that moment of weakness all else had followed. That *yes* had made it her fault as much as his, her sin. That's what he had said, all those many evenings when he'd sat across the family room, ignoring his wife who ignored him in return, and focused his blazing, relentless eyes on her. All those nights . . . All those nights when she'd lived the reality that would later become her nightmares.

Eleven

Christopher waited until they were all on board the homeward-bound ferry before he pulled Lucas aside on a pretext.

"Okay, what's the deal?" Christopher demanded.

"What do you mean?" Lucas stared at him blankly.

"I mean the way Aisha and Zoey have been treating me all night," Christopher said, glancing across the darkened deck to see that Aisha and Zoey were still well out of range.

Lucas shrugged. "Zoey's been ragging me since yesterday about this dumb nomination thing. That's probably what you're picking up on. Has nothing to do with you, man."

"No, that's not it. I've been going for lip and getting cheek all night from Aisha. She's pissed and I don't know why."

"You could ask her," Lucas pointed out.

"I don't think so," Christopher said. He hunched his shoulders. "Zoey tell you where she went this afternoon?"

"I think she did," Lucas said, scrunching his forehead pensively. "I mean, I guess she did, but I don't—"

"Did she go to the mall?"

"Actually, yeah. At least in last period she said she and Eesh and maybe Nina were going to head out to the mall. I remember now because she wanted to know if I wanted to go with them."

"Damn," Christopher said, slamming his hand back against the rail and instantly regretting it when a jolt of pain shot up his arm.

"Like I'd want to go shopping," Lucas said, laughing at the thought. "I think she was just being polite. I don't think she really wanted me along. Unless maybe it would give her more time to make snide remarks about—" He fell silent, looking sideways at Christopher. "What's the matter?"

"I have a bad feeling Aisha saw something she wasn't supposed to see," Christopher said in a low voice.

Lucas leaned closer. "Yeah? What?"

Christopher hesitated. Was Lucas the kind of guy who told his girlfriend everything? Lots of guys were that way, and whatever he told Zoey would go straight back to Aisha. Then he grinned wryly. Hell, Lucas had done time. He probably knew how to keep a secret. "There was this babe—"

"Uh-oh," Lucas commented, glancing over his shoulder guiltily.

Christopher couldn't help but grin. "Blond hair down to her ass," he said. "I mean, major babe. Major, major stuff."

"Oh. You think Aisha caught you looking?"

"I was looking, all right."

Lucas shook his head. "Girls never understand that we *have* to look. We *have* to. It doesn't mean we're going to do anything about it. And the thing is, girls look, too; they're just quicker. They're subtle; just a glance and boom—they've memorized everything down to whether the guy has clean fingernails. Guys, it takes longer. We have to give it a good five- or six-second look."

"See, you're right about that," Christopher said, nodding his agreement.

"And then the girl gives the guy a hard time even though she's just doing the same exact thing, only faster."

"Well, this girl definitely took more than a five- or six-second look," Christopher said.

Lucas grinned wolfishly. "Uh-huh."

"I got her phone number."

The grin on Lucas's face evaporated. "You did what?"

"I got her phone number. I told her I'd call her sometime."

"That's going a long way past looking," Lucas said.

Was it just Christopher's imagination or was Lucas looking disapproving? More likely jealous. "She was into it; what was I supposed to do? Just walk on past and go buy my socks?"

Lucas made a *don't-ask-me* face.

"Give me a break," Christopher said. "Are you

125

telling me you wouldn't have done the same thing?''

"I might have wanted to," Lucas admitted.

"Right."

"But . . . Wait, it's not my business how you and Aisha work things out."

"Look, I'm into Aisha; she's incredible. But you know, I'm not ready to let her nail my feet to the floor. I'm a man. A man is an animal who is made to roam. It's unnatural for a man to limit himself to one female."

"How about one female at a time?" Lucas said dryly.

"Are you telling me you're not going to try and get a little extra on the side? You're going to be totally, one hundred percent faithful to Zoey?"

"That's the plan," Lucas said.

Christopher looked at him in amazement. "The world is full of women, Lucas. Maybe you were in jail too long to remember, but they come in all types and varieties. Tall ones, short ones, small, medium, large and extra large, blond, brunette, redhead, black, white, Asian. I mean, it's like you're saying here you are—you're what, eighteen?—and you're never going to eat anything but the same old meal every day and never try something different?''

"How about if it's my favorite meal?"

"How would you know for sure?"

"I know," Lucas said with a smug little smile that annoyed Christopher unreasonably.

"I guess we're different people," Christopher said, giving Lucas a deprecating look.

"I guess so," Lucas agreed. "I understand what you're saying, though. I do. The only thing is, does Aisha understand all this? I mean, shouldn't you be up front if you're not ready to make some big commitment?"

"She understands," Christopher said uncertainly.

"Then why is she upset?"

"I don't know," Christopher said in sudden frustration. "Look, I never said I was in love with her or anything. She never said she was in love with me, either. If that was how it was I might say, okay, I have to completely ignore other girls. Right?"

"Don't ask me, man," Lucas said. "I deal with things my way; you do whatever you want. I'm no example for anyone to follow. I'm only saying you have to try not to hurt Aisha, because she's not someone you just dump on."

"I'm not going to hurt her," Christopher said, trying to sound confident. "I'll work up something very romantic for Aisha. She'll forget all about it."

He stuck his hand in his pocket and felt the torn slip of paper where he had written the blond girl's number. Her name was Angela. If he called her and went out with her, he'd have to be very careful, because Lucas was right—he didn't want to hurt Aisha.

Nina

Dream number one is the worst.

Dream number one has no pictures and no story. It only has feelings. It only has pain and guilt and shame. Dream number one makes my skin crawl. It makes me feel like I'm choking, like I can't breathe, can't breathe, can't breathe, can't breathe no matter how I try I can't breathe, till I feel I may pass out or die, till my lungs are empty like flattened paper bags and my throat is convulsing and still I can't breathe.

Waking up is just as bad because I remember it so vividly, like it just happened, just then. Like he might still be there in the dark. I'm shaking. My insides are quivering. I feel like my entire body has been rubbed with sandpaper so that I'm tender, raw, even the sheets burn me.

The rest of the day after I have this dream I feel that way. On edge. Raw.

My friends just think of it as one of my occasional bitchy moods. They chalk it up to PMS. I tell them I've had too much coffee. All day long I feel like I have to gulp air, like I have to fill my lungs to bursting on every breath.

I know what this dream means, too. But it's not something I can talk about. *Ever.* Talking would only make it real, and I try very hard to convince myself that it is no longer anything but a dream.

Twelve

Zoey was opening the gate to the Geigers' front yard when a movement high up caught her eye. She shielded her eyes from the morning sun and gazed up at the widow's walk, high atop the third story of the house. Claire was up there, wrapped in a heavy, sky-blue silk robe. Her long black hair rustled in the cool breeze and she was sipping a mug of something hot enough to steam.

"Claire!" she yelled up.

"What on earth are you doing already dressed and running around this early on a Saturday morning?" Claire asked, looking down from her Olympian height.

"I came to see if Nina—and you—wanted to do anything today."

"Like what?"

"I have to get our car washed, and I'm supposed to pick up a package over at the main post office. Then I'm free to do whatever."

"What would whatever be?"

Zoey realized her neck was cricked from looking up. "Shop. Go for a drive somewhere."

"It sounds fascinating," Claire said, grinning at her own sarcasm. "But I think I'll pass. Go ahead and come in. Don't knock; Janelle is baking and it would just make her cranky to answer the door." She gave a little wave and backed out of sight.

Zoey climbed the porch stairs and opened the heavy front door. She was pretty sure Nina would still be asleep, so, feeling playful, she headed upstairs, intending to give Nina a nice, rude awakening.

She grabbed the handle of Nina's bedroom door, prepared to burst in screaming her head off and watch Nina flounder around. But the door resisted. She rattled the doorknob and gave it a push. It still wouldn't open.

"NO, NO, NO!"

The cry through the door was bloodcurdling. Nina's voice, only transformed into something inhuman.

"Nina, it's me, Zoey!" Zoey cried, pressing her ear to the door and rattling the handle again. "It's me, Zoey—are you all right?"

She heard a deep, profound sigh and a few low, muttered curses that sounded more relieved than angry. After a few seconds Zoey heard a metallic scraping through the door. It opened on a rumpled, annoyed-looking Nina, hair sticking out in every direction, the waffle pattern of a blanket pressed into her left cheek. But Nina's eyes didn't match the rest of the look. They were wide, alert, like she had been scared.

132

"Are you aware that it's morning?" Nina asked gruffly.

"I came by to see if you wanted to do anything today." Zoey peered closely at her friend. "Are you okay?"

"The next ferry's not for two hours," Nina pointed out. "I could have slept for those two hours." She backed away from the door and flopped backward on her bed.

Zoey followed her into the room. "I know. That's how long it usually takes to get you going on a Saturday A.M." She ran her fingers over the lock on the door. "What's this for?"

"It's a vain attempt to keep people from waking me up too early," Nina said balefully.

"Ha ha. No, seriously."

Nina sat up and gave a little shrug. "What are we doing today?"

"Washing my parents' car?" Zoey said. "And then I thought maybe we'd drive down to Portland. Experience a different mall for a change. Also I was going to hit the Braille bookstore there for Benjamin."

"Is Benjamin coming?" Nina asked.

"No. Just us girls. I asked Claire, but she wasn't into it. I tried Aisha, but she has to do some stuff for her mom. Get some rooms ready."

Nina stood up, suddenly interested. "Hey, how much does Mrs. Gray charge for those rooms?"

"Lots, I think," Zoey said. "They're very nice. Aisha said they may be in one of those magazines that do inns and bed-and-breakfasts."

"Like hundreds of bucks, I wonder?"

"Why, you want to get away from it all for a night?" Zoey joked.

But Nina didn't smile. "Maybe."

"You're serious. You want to rent a room at the Grays' inn for a night?"

"Maybe several nights," Nina said seriously. Then she smiled. "We have some relatives coming to visit."

"Oh."

"My aunt and her husband."

"You don't like them?"

"What is there to like?"

Zoey's attention was drawn back to the clumsily installed lock on Nina's door. What was going on with Nina? She'd been off for days, it now seemed to Zoey. More angry, more edgy than she usually was. Greater than usual annoyance with her sister, the scene in the lunchroom. Nothing big, really, nothing you could put your finger on. "Hey, were you having a nightmare when I knocked?"

The look on Nina's face was telling. Her eyes narrowed, her face fell. Then, with what looked like a deliberate act of will, she reconstructed her usual cocky, ironic expression. "Yeah," she said. "I had this terrible dream someone was waking me up too early. I'll go take a quick shower," she added before Zoey could interrupt. She grabbed a few items of clothing from her closet and dresser and at least one from a pile on the floor and disappeared in the direction of the bathroom.

Zoey sat on the bed and looked up quizzically

at Trent Reznor on a wall poster. "Is she all right?" she asked Trent. "Of course, you're just the guy to ask."

She glanced at her watch and looked around for something to read to pass the time. She slid open the drawer of Nina's nightstand and froze.

A small but wicked-looking knife lay on top of an aging picture of a ten- or twelve-year-old girl.

A nightmare? A lock? A knife? A semi-serious question about staying at Aisha's?

Zoey pulled out the photo and checked the back. "Nina, eleventh birthday," she read. She replaced it under the knife, feeling deeply troubled.

Suddenly it was as if she could sense something terrible in this familiar room. Something was the matter with Nina. It seemed impossible, but for some reason Nina, fearless, in-your-face Nina, was very afraid.

By early afternoon Zoey had picked up the package at the post office and run the car through the car wash, deftly putting off the flirtatious guy who vacuumed the interior, and made the drive down to Portland. Portland was not especially exciting, being basically just a larger Weymouth, which was in turn just a larger North Harbor. But it had a bookstore with a few shelves of books in Braille. And in any event, it wasn't quite the same old places and faces as home.

"Master and Commander," Nina read the printed title. "Sounds like something Benjamin might like. It's about ships and war."

"Grab it," Zoey said. "What do you think about *Winter's Tale*?"

"Never heard of it," Nina said. "What's it about?"

Zoey pulled out the huge volume and read the blurb. "Mmm, a magic flying horse and a girl with tuberculosis."

Nina laughed. "Benjamin doesn't like magic."

Zoey made a face. "Now, how would you know whether Benjamin likes magic?"

"I do read to him," Nina said.

"And you think he likes ships and war but not magic horses and wasting diseases?"

"He totally prefers war to illness," Nina said confidently. "He's a guy, you know. Ships, planes, guns, wars, adventure, spies, detectives. No magic horses or girls with tuberculosis. Now, *I* might read a book about a magic horse with tuberculosis, but it's not a guy book."

"Suddenly you're the big expert on guys?" Zoey said, teasing innocently. But she saw Nina's jaw clench up. "Nina, I was just teasing," Zoey said placatingly.

"I know," Nina said, paying close attention to the books and refusing eye contact.

They paid for two books, using Zoey's mother's Visa card, and walked in strained silence back to the spot where the car was parked. "Love that clean car smell," Zoey said on opening the door.

Nina nodded distractedly.

Zoey shook her head and started the engine. They drove to the freeway and took the ramp heading back north. Zoey made several more attempts to engage Nina in conversation but gave up after the fifth or sixth uninterested grunt. She reached for the radio and turned it on loud.

Nina clicked it off.

Zoey turned on her, ready to lash out angrily at Nina's sullen mood. But Nina was staring grimly straight ahead, and Zoey subsided.

"Look," Nina said at last, "I'm not a lesbian, all right?"

"I didn't say you were," Zoey said. "Not that it would matter to me."

"Well, I'm not," Nina said. She turned the radio back on and dug a cigarette out of her purse.

This time Zoey turned the radio down. "Listen, Nina, we're best friends, aren't we?"

"That depends on whether you're getting ready to bug me," Nina said through clenched teeth. She was twisting her fingers together and biting the end of the unlit cigarette.

"Why did you put a lock on your door?"

"I just felt like it."

Now Nina had begun to rock, just slightly, forward and back, like a person impatient to get away.

"You have a knife in your nightstand."

"What the hell were you doing in my nightstand?" Nina shouted, horrified.

"Nina, something is scaring you."

"*You're* scaring me, Zo, going through my stuff."

"What's going on?"

"Will you shut up and just drive?" Nina snapped viciously.

Zoey recoiled. She had known Nina nearly all her life and had seen every mood she had. This was not part of any normal mood. Nina's anger had always been weary, or ironic. This was fresh and violently intense.

They drove in silence for a while longer, Nina still twisting her fingers together, still nearly bouncing up and down in her seat. Zoey went over every clue in her mind—the lock, the nightmarish cry, the knife, the photo of Nina five years earlier.

Five years? That was when Nina's mother had died. Was it about that somehow?

Ahead she saw the off-ramp for a rest area. She veered onto it.

"What are we doing?" Nina demanded.

Zoey didn't answer. She slowed and pulled the car into a parking space and turned off the engine. She turned sideways in her seat. "Nina, you are my best friend in the world. I think you—"

"Leave me alone! Leave me alone! Goddamn it, you think you know everything? Just stay out of it!" Nina was shouting, a deafening noise in the enclosed car.

"I can't stay out of it!" Zoey yelled back, fueled by fear and frustration.

Nina's face suddenly twisted, like some huge wrenching sob was working its way through her features. Her eyes were wide, helpless. "Look," she said, mastering herself with difficulty. "I know you're trying to be nice." Nina seemed to be gasping for breath, pausing to suck in several deep, straining lungfuls of air. "Just . . . just leave it alone. There's nothing you can do."

Zoey took Nina's hand. Nina shook it off. "If you are my friend, Zoey, drop it," Nina pleaded.

Zoey hesitated. This wasn't even Nina. Not as she had ever known Nina to be. This was someone new. Someone deformed by terror. A thrill of fear tingled up Zoey's spine.

Zoey bit her lip and reached out, deliberately taking Nina's hand again. Again Nina shook it off. Zoey could see tears welling up in Nina's eyes. Nina flung open the door and ran.

Zoey ran after her, across the grass, past the brick rest rooms and the glass-covered maps of Maine, and on to the edge of the woods. There Nina collapsed, coming to a stop by a picnic table.

Zoey approached quietly, like she would a frightened deer.

Nina laughed, a sad, faint sob. "I can't exactly walk home from here, can I?"

Zoey sat down beside her, and for a third time took her friend's hand. This time Nina didn't resist.

Nina sighed shakily. "I told you my aunt and uncle were coming, right?"

"You mentioned it."

Nina nodded. "Yeah. Well, you remember back when my mom . . . back . . ."

"When your mom died?" Zoey finished softly.

Nina nodded mutely. "Yeah. Well, remember my dad said I should go stay with my aunt and uncle for a while?"

"I never understood that," Zoey said regretfully.

"I was real close to my mom," Nina said in a voice drenched in sadness. "He . . . my dad . . . he thought I needed to get away. Stay with my aunt and uncle. Change of scene and all."

Zoey said nothing. Facts were coming together slowly in her mind, coalescing to form the rough outlines of a picture.

"This has to be a secret," Nina said, her tone now more solid, almost devoid of emotion, flat. "I mean, you have to swear. It doesn't matter if you don't believe me, because I know you won't. But you can't tell anyone."

Zoey felt trapped. She had the awful feeling that what Nina was preparing to tell her should never be kept secret. But she had to honor Nina's wishes, too. "I'll never tell anyone."

"You swear."

"Yes. I swear. And I will believe you."

Nina nodded slowly for a long time. When at last she spoke, it was in a voice Zoey had never heard.

"I was at my aunt and uncle's house for two months. I was eleven. My uncle, he started off just kissing me. Then it was more."

Zoey felt her heart stop.

"Almost every night, for two months . . . He would come into my room. Into my . . . into my bed."

Thirteen

Jake pulled the white face mask down and pinched it over his nose. He lifted the heavy sander and pulled the trigger. It whined furiously, then changed to a lower, harsher pitch as he pressed the spinning belt against the wooden hull of the boat towering above him. Sawdust flew and collected on the plastic lenses of his safety goggles. It gave off a sour, burning smell.

After a while he stopped, lowered the sander, and ran his hand over the surface, feeling the smoothness. That would just about do it, he decided. He'd finish up with a finer-grade sandpaper by hand, and the repair would be ready for the coats of sealer and paint.

He set down the sander and wiped the sweat from his brow with the back of his hand. His father paid him eight dollars an hour to work for him in the marina, which was good money, but his dad always got his money's worth.

Jake glanced longingly at the water, sparkling cool, just a few feet away from the dry dock. He bent over and rummaged his watch from the pocket of his discarded shirt. Good enough. He had put in five solid hours, an hour more than he had promised, and the job had gone well.

He unlaced his heavy work boots and pulled off his socks. He was wearing raggedy cutoffs, which wouldn't be harmed by a little salt water. He walked to the end of the first pier and looked around. A scattering of people lying out on Town Beach to his left. The ferry halfway back to Weymouth.

He took a deep breath and dove in. He opened his eyes under the water and looked up at the gently rocking hulls of the boats tied to the pier. With several kicks he was out in deeper water and coming up for air.

The water was cold as always but invigorating, not numbing. He looked around, deciding which direction to go. The swell was gentle out beyond the breakwater, and somehow the confines of the harbor just didn't seem wide enough. He'd swim up around to the north point, maybe take a rest at the lighthouse. On the way he could check out the sailboat from Bar Harbor that had stopped on its way down the coast to Newport.

He swam hard, enjoying the feeling of his muscles burning while his skin cooled and the sweat and sawdust were washed away. He paused when he reached the beautiful fifty-four footer, rolling at anchor in the middle of the harbor. A look told him the owner and crew were probably ashore—the dinghy was gone. He hailed it anyway, yelling, "Hey, anyone aboard?" No answer.

Too bad; he'd have liked to look around inside. She had an opulent yet professional look about her. He took several deep breaths, then dived under, thinking to get a look at the keel. But something hanging underwater from the anchor line caught his eye. He swam over to it and smiled. Three six-packs of Killian's Red, hanging in a net bag to keep cool.

He started to swim away, intending to head on toward the point, but something stopped him. He looked back at the beer. *They'd never know*, he thought.

But just behind that thought came the angry denial. No way. He didn't steal.

Although it would certainly save money over what he'd have to pay Dave Voorhies for the use of his fake ID. He turned and kicked toward the bag. It would be no problem, and no one would ever know.

His lungs began to burn and he broke the surface, looking around guiltily. No, this was dumb. First of all, he didn't need any more beer. What he needed was to get himself in shape physically and get his concentration back. Beer wouldn't help either of those goals.

He began swimming north at full speed, stretching his muscles, and as his head came up for each breath he checked his progress against the shoreline.

Start stealing beer and you'll end up no better than Lucas, he warned himself. *No better than Lucas?* he repeated ironically. *You need to update your thinking there, Jake. You don't have much reason to look down on Lucas anymore. It's Claire who is the guilty one. Claire.*

Claire, who you can't stop thinking of. Claire, who had gotten away with everything, the only one unhurt. The untouchable, unreachable Claire.

He began inscribing an arc on the surface of the water, now breasting the heavier chop of the more open sea, fighting the current that resisted his advance. The lighthouse on its tiny island of tumbled rock came into view, a squat white-and-black structure.

He had to swim around the islet to reach the tiny sand-and-pebble landing. He drew himself up, fighting the heavy gravitational pull of the water, and threw himself back on a tuft of sea grass. A hundred yards across the water stood the row of restored homes that had once belonged to the whaling captains who operated out of Chatham Island. It was the quaint sort of picture that appealed to tourists. But it was one particular home that drew Jake's eye.

He realized he was disappointed not to see her up on her widow's walk. Still, she could be inside, right up there beneath the sloping roof, behind those twin dormers.

Claire.

Claire, who said she loved him.

The only way he had of making her pay was to be cold, make her feel at least some tiny bit of rejection for once in her charmed life. She wanted to gain total absolution from him for the damage she had done. At least he could deny her that. He could use that one small area of vulnerability to hurt her. He owed Wade that much. He owed it to his dead brother to at the very least not forgive the girl who had killed him.

That was the very, very least he had to do.

A motorboat roared past, halfway to land, bouncing and sending up a high wake. Someone onboard gave a wave and a faint yell. He waved back compliantly, having no idea who they might be.

Again he checked the still-empty widow's walk.

Wade would have ridiculed him for being a wuss. He could imagine Wade's words, hear his contemptuous voice—Man, Jake, you pathetic little wimp. You're so whipped by this babe you'd sell out your own brother. You were ready to try to make Lucas Cabral pay, but now that it's Claire, oh, that's totally different.

It couldn't be different. He had to be true to the memory of Wade. He was sure of that.

A flutter of movement on the widow's walk. His heart leapt. Claire!

But then the movement resolved itself into white wings, and the sea gull flew away.

Aisha knocked on the front door of Christopher's building precisely at six o'clock that evening. It was a huge, rambling, and somewhat rundown Victorian rooming house that fronted the landward side of the island.

When after several minutes no one answered, she cautiously opened the door and went inside. She'd been to Christopher's apartment only once, but she remembered he was on the third floor.

"Hello?" she called out to the gloomy foyer. Somewhere a radio was playing country music, but that didn't sound like Christopher. "Okay," she said. "Let's just hope none of the members of the Addams Family are home right now."

She climbed the stairs and easily found Christopher's door. He had the room on the top floor of an octagonal tower. Not huge, but very distinctive and with amazing views of the beach. She knocked. "Christopher?"

The door opened and there he stood, dressed in a suit coat and tie. Also in black spandex shorts, a mesh T-shirt, and white Nikes. The coffee table was decorated with a candle stuck in an empty bottle of Dr Pepper. The stereo was playing softly.

"Welcome," Christopher said very formally, "to my humble abode."

Aisha gave him a skeptical look but went inside. "Candlelight?"

"I'm fixing you a gourmet dinner," he said, taking her hand and leading her to a pile of pillows stacked together before the table. "Paella."

"Pa-what?"

"Paella. Chicken, sausage, clams, shrimp, and calamari on saffron rice. Very Spanish."

"Oh, that's right. I don't know why I should be surprised. You do cook for a living. At least part of your living."

"I can make anything that's on the menu at Passmores'," Christopher said, heading toward the

146

minuscule kitchen—really just a glorified hot plate with a tiny sink and ancient refrigerator. "In fact, this would cost you seventeen ninety-five down at work. Plus tax and tip."

Aisha laughed. "I like your outfit. I would have dressed up more if I'd realized this was such a formal date."

"Oh, this old thing?"

"Very distinguished. I like the tie and T-shirt look."

"You want some wine with dinner?" he asked. He reached into the refrigerator and came up with a bottle of 7-Up. "We have white and"—he produced a Dr Pepper—"brown."

"I think white wine with seafood," Aisha said. She took the drink and watched as he lifted the lid from a casserole, letting a cloud of fragrant steam escape.

"There are appetizers over on the buffet table."

Aisha looked around the room and spotted a plate of food on his nightstand. "The buffet table? What do you call the bed? Never mind," she added quickly. She lifted a stuffed mushroom cap from the plate and popped it into her mouth. "Hey, this is delicious."

"Six ninety-five, plus tax and tip," he said over his shoulder.

She took a swallow of her soda and eyed his back contentedly. Tall, dark, handsome. Hardworking and ambitious. Smart, funny, sexy, and he could cook paella and mushrooms stuffed with crab. What exactly had she been thinking when she'd tried to get rid of him? He was like a text-book example of the perfect guy. If you looked *Mr. Right* up in a dictionary, they'd have a picture of Christopher Shupe.

It wasn't like she was just falling victim to hormones or some stupid crush based on the fact that he had a nice body. This was a perfectly sensible thing. It was logical. He was a great guy, no matter how critical you wanted to be.

As long as you overlooked the fact that he had a weak memory when it came to where he bought socks.

"Okay," Christopher said, quickly filling a couple of plates and tossing on a garnish, "sit."

She sat on the pillows and crossed her legs. Christopher put a steaming plate of food down before her, and one for himself. He sat down and raised his soda. "A toast. To Aisha, which means 'life.' "

"And Christopher," she said.

"Which means?" he prompted.

Aisha smiled. It seemed like a long time ago that he had told her that the day would come when *Christopher* would mean "boyfriend." She had told him there was no way, but even then, his confidence had half convinced her. "To Christopher," she said, clinking her bottle against his. "Which, to my surprise, really does mean boyfriend."

"Okay, now eat. Don't let my great food get cold."

She dived in. "Hey. This really is fantastic."

"Maybe I should blow off college and go to the

Culinary Institute instead," he suggested. "Everyone who graduates from there has like five solid job offers waiting when he comes out."

"You could do both. An MBA and a cooking degree? Could be deadly if you want to run a restaurant."

"You know something?" he said, narrowing his eyes shrewdly. "That's not a bad idea. I can see a whole nationwide chain, hundreds of restaurants—Shupe's International House of Paella."

"That way you could use your business degree to figure out what to charge."

The telephone rang.

Christopher rolled his eyes. "Don't people realize I'm trying to seduce a woman here?"

"Oh, is *that* what you're trying to do?"

"Remember before, when I mentioned the tip?" He gave her an exaggerated leer and got up to get the telephone on the third ring. "Shupe's International House of Paella," he answered. He listened for a second and immediately his voice dropped. Not quite a whisper, just a low pitch intended to make it hard for Aisha to overhear his conversation. With the music from the stereo, she could make out very little.

But she could hear the tone of his voice.

He came back after a minute. "I took it off the hook so we won't be disturbed again."

"Anyone I know?" Aisha asked nonchalantly.

He shook his head dismissively. "An old guy I do some landscaping for. He wanted to know if I could put in some rosebushes for him. This time of year? Rosebushes?''

Aisha smiled for his benefit. *You are such a liar, Christopher. Such a quick, professional liar. Was it the girl with the long blond ponytail? Or some other girl? Because it certainly wasn't an old man you were using that voice on.*

"You work too much," she said.

"I know," he said, reaching to take her hand. "Too little time for what's important. Like being with you."

The amazing thing was, he still seemed totally sincere, Aisha noted. And the worst thing was that her insides still quivered helplessly at the touch of his hand on hers. It was terrible how much she wanted him, even now, even knowing.

Right guy or wrong guy. It was too late for her to push him away.

She used to laugh at Zoey for being a hopeless romantic.

Now it turns out I'm just as dumb as Zoey, after all, Aisha thought sadly.

Fourteen

Benjamin fingered the titles of the books Zoey had brought him and set them down on a ledge inside his oak rolltop desk. The desk had tons of cubbyholes of different sizes and shapes, which made it perfect for Benjamin, who could find things only by remembering exactly where he had left them. It also had wood of a wonderful texture that was a pleasure to run his hands over.

He heard a tapping sound, fingers on glass. Left window, he decided, orienting himself by the desk and aiming his sunglasses in that direction. The tapping came again, followed by a voice he recognized as belonging to Lucas.

"Ben, it's me, man."

Benjamin pondered for a moment why Lucas would come tapping at his window and speaking in a loud whisper, but really, the reason was somewhat obvious—it could only have to do with Zoey.

He felt for the window latch, opened it, and raised the window. A whiff of cool breeze met his face.

"Is there some good reason why you don't just

go to the front door?'' Benjamin asked.

"Your sister," Lucas said, sounding exasperated. "Is she really pissed at me or what?"

"You think I'm dumb enough to get in the middle of you and Zoey having a lovers' quarrel? Do I look that stupid?"

"You don't have to get in the middle," Lucas said quickly. "It's just that we were supposed to go out tonight and she called a few minutes ago and said she wanted to cancel because she wasn't feeling well."

"Uh-huh."

"So is she really not feeling well, or is she blowing me off over this dumb-ass homecoming crap? I mean, that would be very petty, in my opinion. But she may have found out what I've been doing."

"What *have* you been doing?" Benjamin asked, against his better judgment.

"I've just been making a few calls. You know, kids from school, telling them not to vote for me or anything."

Benjamin laughed, delighted. "Only you, Lucas."

"I think maybe Zoey found out and that's why she won't go out tonight."

Benjamin shrugged. "All I can tell you is she went shopping down in Portland with Nina and when she came back, she was very quiet. She sounded like she might not be feeling well."

"Really?"

"I only know what I hear."

"Huh. Well, maybe it's one of those female things."

"Maybe. Or else she hates your guts," Benjamin added helpfully. "Maybe she's found another guy. Could be up in her room with him right now."

"Thanks a lot," Lucas said sarcastically. "I'm giving you the finger, by the way."

Benjamin grinned and shut the window. Lucas was a relief, after Zoey going out with straight-arrow Jake for so long. He could get along with Lucas. Lucas had an edge of larceny in his soul.

How on earth was *Claire* ever going to have a relationship with Jake? The question popped into his mind, bringing with it a renewed dose of the sadness he'd carried with him ever since Claire and he had broken up.

He tried to push the thought aside. He couldn't spend his life crying over Claire. He sighed and thought about his sister instead. Was Zoey sick? Or was she really just giving Lucas a hard time?

He opened the door and climbed the stairs to Zoey's room. "Hey, Zo. You in there?"

"Yeah."

She sounded dispirited, depressed maybe. Or else like he had just woken her up from a nap. "Can I talk to you for a second? Can I come in?"

"Sure."

He went in and stopped after two steps, waiting for her to speak so he could locate her.

"What do you want?" Zoey asked, not rude but distracted. She was on her bed.

"I just had a visit from Lucas. He wanted to

know if you were sick or something."

"I'm not sick," Zoey said.

But not exactly happy, either, Benjamin noted. "Are you okay?"

"Uh-huh."

"Uh-huh," Benjamin echoed disparagingly.

"Look, it's just something, all right?"

He shrugged. "Whatever you say." He started to leave, but she spoke again, sounding distant and strange.

"Can I ask your advice on something?"

Benjamin winced involuntarily. "My advice?"

"It's kind of a philosophical question, you know," Zoey said.

"You sure I'm the right person to ask?"

"I don't know who else to ask," Zoey said flatly.

Benjamin located the chair by her dormer desk and sat down. "Okay, shoot."

Zoey was silent for a while. "Which is better—keeping your promise to a friend, or breaking the promise if you think your friend needs help?" she finally asked.

Benjamin ran his hand through his hair. "Is that all you're going to tell me?"

"It's all I *can* tell you."

"Hmm. Let's see, is it a matter of life or death?"

"I don't think so, but it's close."

"Really," Benjamin said, suddenly feeling a premonition of some unhappiness. Zoey wasn't being Zoey. This was as grim as he had ever heard her. Who was the friend? Lucas? He hadn't seemed

154

worried. Nina? When had Nina ever worried about anything serious? "If this friend is able to make his or her own decisions, then I guess you have to let them," Benjamin said uncertainly. "I guess that means if they want you to keep a secret, you have to keep a secret. Unless it's a crime or something," he added as an afterthought.

"Unless it's a crime," Zoey repeated thoughtfully.

"Jeez, I don't know, Zoey. I'm not a philosopher."

"I know."

"Can you at least tell me who we're talking about?" Benjamin asked.

"I haven't decided that yet," Zoey said. "I haven't decided what to do."

"You'll figure out the right answer," Benjamin said reassuringly. He got up to leave. When he was halfway out the door, Zoey spoke again.

"There are some real creeps in the world, aren't there?"

Her venom surprised Benjamin. "Are there?" he asked.

"Thanks for talking to me," Zoey said.

Benjamin heard her close the door behind him.

"Go away."

"It's me," Claire said.

"I know, that's why I said go away."

"I'm on a mission from Dad," Claire said, trying to remain patient. She heard a metallic scrape and the door opened suddenly.

"What?"

Claire stared at her sister. Nina's eyes were vacant and red-rimmed, as if she'd been crying. "What's the matter with you?"

"Nothing's the matter with me," Nina said shortly. Then she relented. "I tried to smoke a cigarette again, and it made my eyes puff up, all right?"

Claire shook her head. "Someday you'll have to explain to me why you would go out of your way to try and become addicted to something every sane person is trying to drop."

"I'm not a sane person," Nina said. "What do you want, anyway?"

"I'm delivering a message. Daddy wants to be sure certain people have their rooms clean for tomorrow."

"My room is clean," Nina snapped.

Claire pushed her way into the room. She looked around, nodding with satisfaction. "Pretty clean by your standards, I'll admit. Although some people think clothing should be in the closet, not on the floor. And some people even believe that sheets should be changed more than once a month."

"Claire, why don't you go jump off your stupid widow's walk and do me and the rest of the world a favor?"

"Look, Nina, I don't give a damn; I'm just delivering the message. You can start a fire in the middle of your floor and roast marshmallows for all I care."

She turned and marched to the door, shaking her

head. Nina seemed to be in a fairly rotten mood, which just exacerbated Claire's own fairly rotten mood. To top it off, their father was also in a fairly rotten mood, brought on by the fact that his Sunday off and several subsequent days were going to be ruined by visiting relatives. Their branch of the Geiger family was not big on backslapping, trading old stories, and forced friendliness. It just brought out the crankiness in them.

Some, apparently, more than others.

"Home alone on a Saturday night, Claire?" Nina took a parting shot.

Claire pressed her lips in a steely smile and turned back to Nina. "Home alone *every* Saturday night, Nina?"

"I've decided to become a nun; what's your excuse?"

"Guys are afraid I have insanity running in my family," Claire said. "And those who have met you are sure of it."

Nina stared at her, presumably readying her return volley. "Who's getting what room?" she asked.

Claire was taken aback. It was a sudden shift of topic, like Nina had just changed the channel without warning. "What?"

"Aunt E. in the back bedroom?" Nina asked, her eyes unfocused, staring into middle space.

"Yes. Are you . . . Are you okay?"

Nina nodded, still staring. "When will they be here?"

"Tomorrow, late morning, around eleven, so

you should consider getting out of bed sometime before then.''

"Yeah,'' Nina said.

Claire started to leave a second time. But even by Nina's standards, she was behaving strangely. "Dad's doing the barbecue cookout thing. He said we can invite people.'' No response, just blank staring and a sort of continuous nodding. "I think Dad just wants people around so he'll have an excuse not to have to talk to Uncle Mark.''

Nina looked up sharply. "He doesn't like Uncle Mark?''

"I guess Uncle Mark always gets defensive because we have money.''

"He does?''

"That's what Dad says. I wouldn't know. I don't think I've seen him since we were little.''

"Did you ever stay at their house?'' Nina asked, her eyes boring into Claire.

Claire shifted uncomfortably. All joking aside, maybe Nina really was becoming a little unbalanced. "No, I never stayed with them. You did, though, right?''

"Uh-huh.''

Claire was losing patience with this weird conversation. Was Nina on drugs or just being strange? "Well, then you'll all have plenty to talk about. Now, um, if you don't mind, I have to return to planet Earth.''

"Bye, Claire,'' Nina said, sounding strangely sad and distant.

The door closed and again Claire heard a metallic scrape.

Fifteen

Nina watched *Saturday Night Live* on the TV in her room until it went off at one. Then she spent the next two hours switching back and forth between MTV, Home Shopping, and reruns on Nick at Night. Nick was doing a *Brady Bunch* marathon.

At three she made an effort to go to sleep, but gave up almost immediately. As soon as the comforting light of the TV screen went off, the walls seemed to close in around her. She switched the TV back on, but nothing held her interest. It had all become just disconnected sounds, shadows marching from left to right, right to left without purpose.

She had known for years this day would come. She had known that she was not really done with the man who had introduced her to shame. He was family, after all. Family. Sooner or later he would reappear, stepping out of her memories and nightmares into her real life again.

She gulped for air, straining for each breath as the memories flowed through her again. There had been pain, yes, but the pain was the easier part. Far worse had been the fact that at times there had been a sickening sort of pleasure, like being tickled and tickled while you screamed and pleaded and the person tickling you wouldn't stop. And afterward he would cry softly and say he was sorry. He was weak, he said, he knew it. But it was her fault, too. It wasn't his fault that she was so sweet and pretty. He couldn't help how he felt. How she made him feel.

And she could never, ever tell anyone, because if she did, no one would believe her. Who would believe a little girl over a grown man? He would tell everyone she was making it up, and people would call her a liar and say she was disgusting and sick. No one would believe her. Ever.

Except . . .

Nina sat up in her bed and pulled her blankets close. Except that she had told someone. Zoey.

And Zoey *had* believed her.

Had Zoey just been pretending to believe? Did she secretly think Nina was crazy or making it all up? She tried to remember everything Zoey had said as they sat by the picnic table, bothered by flies and the smell of garbage spilling out of the cans. Had she been just pretending?

No. Zoey had never lied to her.

Zoey *had* believed her.

No one would ever believe her, but Zoey had.

She jumped up and began dressing with hurried, clumsy fingers. There was one place she could go, and one person she could talk to.

It took ten minutes to dress, creep down the

160

stairs, and emerge into a foggy night of silent streets and dark windows. She walked along Lighthouse, listening to the surf on the rocks and the impatient rustle of the trees that lined the street. She turned down Camden, past closed shops and colorful window displays that were all shades of gray, her steps loud on brick sidewalks and cobblestoned streets.

Zoey's house was as dark as everything else. No porch light, no glimmer of illumination escaped through drawn curtains and shades.

Nina knelt by the low landing of the front door and ran her fingers slowly over dirt and twigs and rocks, searching. It took several tries before she felt the right rock and picked it up. In the bottom of the rock was a sliding panel that concealed the Passmores' extra key. Nina had seen Zoey resort to it on several occasions.

Feeling frightened, but so much less frightened than she had in her own home, Nina used the key to open the front door. She closed it gently behind her, wincing at the click of the tumblers as she locked it again.

Up the stairs and she was at Zoey's door.

Now the only problem is keeping Zoey from screaming, Nina realized with some return of her usual good humor. *She'll wake up and see me and either think I'm a burglar or that I really am gay.*

She opened Zoey's door stealthily and stepped into the room. The only sound was Zoey's heavy breathing. Nina crept forward and stood by the bed.

She touched Zoey's shoulder.

"Unh," Zoey murmured.

"Wake up," Nina said. "It's me, Lucas. I have to have you."

It took several seconds, but Zoey's eyes opened at last. She blinked, squinted, blinked again.

"It's me, Nina."

"Nina?" A voice blurry with sleep and incomprehension.

"Yeah. I'm afraid so. It's three forty. In the morning. Or night."

"Nina?" More coherent this time.

Zoey's next question would be what the hell was she doing creeping into her bedroom in the middle of the night. Only Zoey didn't ask the question. She sat up and flicked on the dim, yellow bulb of her nightstand light. She was wearing a Boston Bruins jersey, twisted about twice around her body.

"I couldn't sleep," Nina admitted, "so I thought I'd make sure you couldn't sleep, either. Sorry."

"Don't be sorry. You're my best friend," Zoey said.

For some reason that simple statement brought tears to Nina's eyes. She tried to toss off some clever line, but the excitement of being out in the night alone had worn off, leaving nothing now but despondency and profound exhaustion.

Zoey leaned toward her and put her arms around Nina's shoulders and hugged her close.

Nina let her head fall onto her friend's shoulder, unable to speak. Unable to offer an explanation that Zoey had not even asked for.

"Take off your shoes," Zoey said. And Nina kicked them off.

Zoey lay back against the pillows and rested Nina's head in the crook of her arm. Nina felt tears running freely, wetting the sleeve of Zoey's jersey. And she felt a tidal wave of weariness sweep over her, paralyzing her limbs, numbing her mind and at last obliterating her consciousness.

An hour later, Zoey gently disentangled herself from Nina and got up from the bed. She needed to think, and she was ravenous. Nina seemed in no danger of waking up. She was in a sleep so deep she might have been in a coma, not even fluttering an eyelid as Zoey left the room.

Zoey padded down the stairs and went into the dark kitchen. Even before she turned on the light, she knew someone was there. And she knew who.

She flicked on the harsh fluorescent light. Benjamin sat there, a Braille book open before him on the table, a bag of Doritos nearby.

"Zoey?" he asked.

"Yes."

"Is Nina with you?"

"No. She's asleep upstairs. How did you know?"

He shrugged. "I heard someone sneaking in. I figured it was Lucas, actually, having the somewhat sleazy imagination I do, but I wanted to be sure it was okay, so I stood outside your door for a while until I heard you say Nina's name."

Zoey opened the refrigerator door and stared in

at the assortment of leftovers, milk, soda, lunch meats, and defrosting chicken. She opened the freezer and lifted the Ben & Jerry's Chunky Monkey. It was at least half full. Good for a start.

She grabbed a spoon from the drawer and sat down at the table across from Benjamin.

"I have the feeling that Nina was the person you were asking all those hypothetical questions about earlier," Benjamin said as Zoey took her first bite.

"I don't think you'd believe me if I denied it," Zoey said.

"No. She's obviously in trouble. Enough trouble to bring her here in the middle of the night. And enough trouble to shake you up badly enough to say 'there are some real creeps in the world.' A very un-Zoey-like thing to say."

"Look, I don't think you want to get involved, Benjamin. It's not your problem. She's *my* best friend."

To Zoey's surprise, Benjamin looked angry. "She's my friend, too," he said. "I care what happens to Nina."

Zoey took another bite, but the ice cream seemed to have lost any flavor. She stared blankly at the toaster for a few minutes, going over all that Nina had told her. Then she snapped back, refocusing on her brother. Nina was carrying a huge load of fear and shame. Even secondhand, even just the part she had shared with Zoey felt crushing.

The decision to tell Benjamin happened before she was consciously aware of it. She simply began talking. "She has an aunt and uncle coming for a visit. They're arriving tomorrow, and this is the aunt and uncle she stayed with right after her mom died.''

Now Zoey hesitated. Nina had sworn her to secrecy. Zoey had given her word. If Nina knew she was telling Benjamin, she would probably be humiliated beyond belief. But this had become Zoey's problem now as well as Nina's. It was too big for Zoey to be sure that her word to Nina was the most important thing.

Benjamin was waiting patiently, unmoving. It brought a smile to Zoey's face. So typically Benjamin. The smile evaporated as she made the final decision. ''Her uncle molested her. Repeatedly.''

Benjamin said nothing, just hung his head.

''I think she's afraid he'll try it again.''

He remained silent, shaking his head almost imperceptibly. When he spoke, it was only to mutter a few unusual obscenities. Then he seemed to refocus on the problem at hand. ''She's older now—she could tell her father.''

''I think it's more complicated than that,'' Zoey said. ''The bad thing is that she feels like she's to blame as much as he is.''

''How the hell would *she* be to blame? She was an eleven-year-old girl. He was an adult.''

''It's how she feels,'' Zoey said helplessly.

''It may be, but she has to realize that's just not the way it is. She was eleven, for God's sake. You can't vote when you're eleven, you can't drink, you can't drive. You can't play the lottery or go on half the rides at Disney World. She was just a kid.

When you're eleven, your only responsibilities are doing your homework and feeding your dog. You don't decide whether or not to have sex.''

"Maybe you should tell Nina that,'' Zoey said.

"Someone should,'' Benjamin said heatedly. "All the right is on Nina's side. All the wrong is on her creep of an uncle's side. All of it. A hundred percent. Goddamnit, she ought to put that son of a bitch in jail.''

"Could she?'' Zoey asked. It hadn't occurred to her that would be an option.

"I don't know,'' Benjamin admitted. "I guess it depends on whether too much time has passed, things like that. I don't know. I don't know if that's what she'd want to do. But it is what should be done. He shouldn't get away with it.''

"I don't think she wants to tell anyone.''

Benjamin nodded. "Yeah, I can imagine.''

"She's worried what people would think.''

Benjamin smiled crookedly. "I didn't think Nina ever worried about what people would think of her.''

"This is pretty major. She doesn't want people staring at her and whispering and saying there goes the girl who was molested by her uncle. Nina doesn't mind people thinking she's strange; she just doesn't want them feeling sorry for her.''

"Tell me about it,'' Benjamin said dryly.

"I don't know what I should do,'' Zoey confessed. "I think someone needs to tell Mr. Geiger about this. And I think Nina should talk to a shrink or a counselor or someone who knows about this kind of stuff."

"And you're wondering if you should be the one who tells?"

"I don't know. What if Nina won't?"

"It would be better if she told," Benjamin said. "I mean, better for her, rather than you or me or someone else doing it. If she decides to tell, it will be like she decided to fight back, you know? Does this guy have kids?"

"No." Zoey shook her head. The same thought had occurred to her. "But there are always other ways for this kind of person."

"Maybe we should ask Mom and Dad," Benjamin suggested.

"I can't do that. I promised Nina. She said she had to have at least one person in the world she could trust."

Benjamin nodded in reluctant agreement. "Well, she has two."

Zoey got up and put the lid back on the half-melted ice cream. "I still don't know what to do."

"Sorry," Benjamin said dispiritedly. "You know, I used to get so pissed at people for feeling sorry for me, for saying poor Benjamin. But now all I can keep thinking is poor Nina."

Zoey smiled sadly at her brother, sitting there with his blank brown eyes filled with tears, staring into the fluorescent glare. "No one says poor Benjamin anymore."

A flicker of a smile. "Damn right," he said.

"I better go back up."

"Yeah. Good luck."

She began to leave but stopped, with her hand on the light switch. "Benjamin?"

"What?"

"I'm very glad I have you as my big brother."

"Don't go all sentimental on me, Zoey."

"Sorry," she said. "Must be the lack of sleep."

"Yeah. Good night. And . . . and I love you, too, Zo."

Claire

I don't know why Nina and I ended up having the kind of relationship we do. You see these families — sisters, brothers, brother-sister combinations of various types — and some are like the Brady Bunch or the Partridge Family, all gooey and close-knit. Others are more your basic Cain and Abel thing.

I guess Nina and I are somewhere in between. We won't be forming a band and going on the road, but at the same time we aren't likely to kill each other.

I haven't really ever thought about it that much, but on those occasions when I do, I wonder if it all goes back to our mom having died. It seems like it was around then that we started sniping at each other a little more.

More likely, though, we are the people we are, and that's all there is to it. Nina is more involved with other people than I am. She's more provocative in some ways. Obviously she's more popular than I'll ever be, at least with other girls. And God knows she's funnier.

When I look at the future, I see Nina maybe doing comedy, blowing away the audience on Letterman. Or else writing funny plays in New York, still with an unlit cigarette hanging out her mouth. Maybe by then she'll have graduated to cigars.

I see myself alone, studying climatol

ogical data in some lonely station in Antarctica, learning to create the computer model that will finally be able to predict weather all over the planet. That would make me happy.

We're different people. I know that doesn't necessarily mean we have to be ragging on each other constantly. But that's the way it's worked out. And it's too late now for either of us to change, or to want to change.

Sixteen

Nina woke to a stiff neck and cold toes. It took a moment or two for her to understand where she was, or to remember why Zoey was sleeping beside her. Clear, morning sunlight spilled around the edges of the curtains on Zoey's side window, threatening to banish the last of night from the room.

She sat up on her elbow and searched for Zoey's clock. Nine fifty. Late for Zoey to be asleep, early for Nina's normal weekend schedule. Poor Zoey. It must not have been a very good night's sleep for her.

Nina lay back down on the pillow. She didn't want to get up. If she got up, she would have to leave, and it was so safe here, so far from everything that awaited her at home. Maybe that was the answer. Maybe she could just stay here until her uncle was gone. Zoey would let her. Zoey was her friend, thank God . . . if there was a God. Zoey had believed her because that's what friends, really close friends, were required to do.

But her uncle's prediction still held true for

everyone else. Claire would never believe her. Claire would accuse her of having made it all up to get attention. And her father . . . like he would tell his sister her husband was a pervert? Not likely.

She heard the pattern of Zoey's breathing change. She was awake.

"Morning," Nina said.

"Mmm. Yeah," Zoey mumbled. She shook her head to clear away the sleep and sat up. "How are you doing?"

"My neck is stuck and my leg is asleep," Nina said. "Can't you get a bigger bed?"

"Sorry, I wasn't expecting guests."

"And your pillows are too soft."

"Oh, it's late," Zoey said, peering at her clock.

"I slept like a rock," Nina confessed.

"Good."

"Yeah. Thanks," Nina said a little sheepishly. "I just hope this never gets out around school. They'd all be *sure* I was gay."

"Look at it as a slumber party," Zoey said. "That's Lucas's line. He keeps saying, 'It wouldn't be like we were sleeping together, Zoey, it would just be a slumber party.'"

Nina nodded, only half listening. "I guess I should get going."

"You don't have to go, Nina," Zoey said. "There's no reason why you can't stay. We'll buy you a toothbrush. You can borrow my clothes."

Nina nearly choked up. She'd been certain Zoey would make the offer. "That's sweet of you, Zo . . ."

"You could read to Benjamin all day long," Zoey proposed, "you know, to earn your rent."

Nina smiled ruefully. "Just what Benjamin would like, another girl around the house using up the hot water and getting in the way."

"He'd like it if you stayed," Zoey said, sounding a little uncomfortable. "Look, I have to tell you something that might make you mad."

"Nothing you could say would make me mad. I owe you big time."

"I, uh, couldn't get back to sleep last night, and when I went downstairs to get some munchies, Benjamin was up. He'd heard you come in."

"Oh, God, you didn't tell him, did you? Oh, God."

"Look, Benjamin is—"

"Oh, you did. You told him." Nina leaned over and held her head in both hands. She wanted to crawl under the bed and disappear. She would never be able to face him again. "He'll think I'm nuts," she moaned. "He's going to think I'm so disgusting now."

Zoey put her hand on Nina's shoulder. "He's not going to think any of that, Nina—you're wrong."

"How could he not?" Nina asked desperately. "I go around saying my uncle and I did all those things together. Oh, God." She gasped for air.

"You didn't do all those things *together*," Zoey said sharply. "He did them to you. *To* you. That's what Benjamin said. He said you were just a kid. You probably couldn't even ride half the rides at Disney World."

"What?" Nina demanded, unable to make sense of what Zoey was saying.

"Look, you were a little kid. You didn't *decide* anything. But you know what? Even if you *had*, Nina. Even if it had all been your idea, and you'd wanted to do it, that still wouldn't change the fact that he was an adult and it was his responsibility."

"I didn't want to," Nina said, blazing suddenly.

"I know you didn't," Zoey said.

"I didn't, but he made me."

"You couldn't stop him. He was older and bigger and stronger. There was nothing you could have done."

Nina hesitated. Nothing she could have done? Of course she could have done . . . something. Something. She could have said no.

But she had said no. Hundreds of times. And she'd cried, and begged.

"There was nothing you could have done, Nina," Zoey repeated. "None of it was your fault."

Nina tried to believe it, but somewhere deep in her mind a voice still said, No, Nina, it *was* your fault. Of course it was your fault. How could it not be? You could have done . . . something.

Yet now there was this new idea, just floating along on the edge of her mind, insubstantial still. Maybe it wasn't her fault. Maybe she couldn't have done anything.

Uncle Mark had said it was her fault. And he'd said that no one would ever believe her.

Only now, Zoey believed her. And so did Benjamin.

"My dad is having a barbecue for them," Nina said. "He said I should invite whoever I wanted."

"You know I'll come if you want," Zoey said. "So will Benjamin."

"If you guys were there, I wouldn't be so . . ." Nina's words were choked off by a fresh wave of emotion.

"Sounds like fun," Zoey said, so gamely that Nina had to laugh through her tears.

"Oh, yeah. Loads of fun."

The island's only grocery store was small, indifferently stocked, and notoriously overpriced. But the alternative was to take a ferry ride to Weymouth, travel by car to the Shop and Save, travel back by car, park, carry a week's groceries from the parking garage onto the ferry, and ride the ferry home. People went through all that to stock up on Cheerios and canned goods and beer, but if you wanted something frozen, or anything in a hurry, the Chatham Island Market was the only choice.

Claire pushed a cart through the aisles, having already picked up the Sunday *New York Times* her father liked to read, a pound of butter for the corn on the cob, and the cider vinegar that was so important to her father's homemade barbecue sauce.

That, along with one or two other items, completed the official list as Janelle and her father had written it. Now she was looking for anything new or interesting, anything she might want for herself.

After all, if she was going to be forced to run down to the grocery store first thing on a Sunday morning, she deserved some sort of reward.

Nina, apparently operating from some sixth sense, had managed to be gone when the chore came up. Very unlike her to be up and about so early on a weekend.

Claire headed toward the front of the store, resigning herself to the fact that nothing else really seemed worth buying. She stopped suddenly as she saw Jake come into the store, heading right to the register where his own family's Sunday *Boston Globe* was on reserve. He was dressed for church. Claire glanced at her watch. She didn't attend church herself, but she was pretty sure the service started in fifteen minutes, meaning Jake had plenty of time. She quickly dropped a big sack of charcoal into the cart and beelined for the register.

"Jake. Hi."

"Oh, hi," he said, seeming a little flustered.

She made a point of straining to lift the charcoal from the basket to the checkout counter. After a fractional hesitation, Jake grabbed the sack and hefted it for her.

"My dad's throwing a barbecue this afternoon," Claire said, pointing to the charcoal as evidence. "We have some relatives coming in. Forgot the charcoal, and now I have to drag that all the way home." She felt a little ridiculous, pulling the old helpless female routine, but then, Jake seemed to be causing her to do all sorts of dumb things she wouldn't normally do.

177

"Yeah, your dad should have come to get it."

Claire shrugged. "I don't think he thought about how heavy it is. Especially with the rest of this stuff."

Jake wrinkled his forehead in a pained expression. "If you're going straight home, I guess I could carry it for you. I mean, I've got ten minutes to spare before the service."

"That would be great," Claire said gratefully. Poor Jake, she reflected, trapped by his own politeness. Although, to be honest, he owed her.

She paid and took the bag containing the food and the newspaper while Jake lifted the charcoal onto his shoulder.

"You know, my dad wanted us to invite some more people to this thing," Claire said.

"Uh-huh."

"It's swordfish and steaks and corn on the cob," she said.

"Sounds good," he said noncommittally.

"I don't suppose you'd come," she half asked.

He shrugged. "I don't know."

"If you want to, I'd like you to. Just as a friend. I promise I won't go around telling people you're my boyfriend or anything if you don't want."

He shifted the bag to his other shoulder. "I don't know what to do," he admitted bleakly.

"About the barbecue?" she asked, deliberately obtuse.

"About you," he said bluntly.

"Oh."

"I think about you a lot."

"Good things?"

"Not always," he said harshly. Then in a softer tone, "Sometimes."

"I'm glad. About the sometimes."

"You'll laugh, but I was actually going to ask my minister about it."

"About me?" Claire said, vaguely threatened by the notion of being discussed with a minister. Was she a moral dilemma now? A sin?

Jake laughed shortly. "He's basically cool for an old guy. And I can't really talk to my dad or mom about things like this."

"You could talk to me," Claire offered.

"You're the problem."

"Oh. That's right. I forgot."

He relented a little. "You're not the *only* problem, all right? You're just one problem."

They had reached the front door of the house. Jake slung the sack down onto the porch steps. Claire brushed charcoal dust from his shoulders.

Both realized at the same moment that they were close, their faces only inches apart.

Claire stopped brushing. He was looking at her with eyes full of doubt and something else. She moved closer, ready if he wanted to make a move, but not wanting to repulse him by being too direct.

"I want to," he whispered.

"Then do," Claire said.

He shook his head. "I don't know. I don't know what's right."

"What's *right*?" she repeated wryly.

"I should hate you," he said.

179

"But you don't."

He looked down at the ground. "No." He turned and began to walk away, slumped as if he were still carrying the heavy sack.

"Come by this afternoon," she called after him. "It's just food. It's not a commitment."

He turned, walking slowly backward. "Steaks, you said?"

"New York strip."

"Let me think about it."

"I'll save you one. Medium rare?"

He started to answer, but at that moment the church's bells began to peal from the direction of the circle. He gave a wave and took off at a run.

Seventeen

Nina passed through the crowd milling around outside the church on her way home from Zoey's. The church did double-duty for Catholics and Protestants, with the Catholics getting the use of the historic building from eight to ten and the Protestants from ten on.

Lucas was just on his way out, along with his mother. Jake and his family and Aisha and her family were heading in. Aisha gave Nina a wave and a helpless shrug as her little brother pushed her toward the door.

Nina walked on, feeling the state that comes after tired. She was moving automatically, like a machine. Her mind was clear, racing at a frantic pace, processing the same information over and over and getting nowhere. What should she do? The question came up again and again and led only back in a circle to itself once more.

She needed a week of sleep. She needed to be far away. She needed to scream at the top of her lungs and shatter anything she could lay her hands on.

Someone had dropped a sack of charcoal on the front steps, and for a moment Nina stared at it as if it might be an omen. But the charcoal held no magic answers.

She went up to her room and sat on her cold bed. It seemed like a lifetime since she had lain in it before running in near panic to Zoey.

She looked at the clock. Ten minutes after ten. The next ferry had already left Weymouth and would be here in fifteen minutes. Fifteen minutes. If her uncle was on that ferry, he would reach the island in fifteen minutes. Two more to disembark. Five more to walk up to the house.

Or would her father go down and meet them?

Nina jumped up and went back out into the hall. "Claire. Are you up there?" she yelled up the stairs.

"Yes. Where have you been? I got stuck going to the store and it was your turn."

"Where's Dad?"

"Down at the ferry meeting Aunt E."

Nina went back into her room. He would be here in a very few minutes. And there was no way she could avoid seeing him again. Saying hello. Even a hug.

She sat down on her bed. If before her mind had been in hyperdrive, it now seemed paralyzed. It was as if she were caught moving in slow motion while the minutes flew past. Now the ferry would be docking, on time as always. Now they would be getting off, calling out to Nina's father. Big hugs for his sister, a handshake for Uncle Mark. How was your trip and oh, it's so beautiful here.

They weren't going to have to drag her from her room unwillingly. She wasn't going to take this like a little kid afraid of the first day of school.

She got up and headed down the stairs, feeling with each step like she was on her way to witness a tragedy she had no power to stop.

She was sitting in the living room when she heard laughing voices coming across the front yard. Closer, closer. The door opened. Her aunt was the first in, then her father, dropping luggage. Uncle Mark stepped in last.

He was shorter than her father, with a doughy complexion and slumping shoulders. But he had beautiful blue eyes that seemed out of place in a man otherwise so ordinary looking.

"Well, here's Nina now," her father announced as if they'd just been discussing her.

Aunt Elizabeth came forward and gave her a hug, making all the usual noises about how she'd grown, how she remembered Nina as a little girl and here she was practically a woman.

Nina felt her aunt release her. She stood there between living room and foyer, not feeling the floor under her feet, aware only of her heart pounding at twice its normal speed.

"Nina probably doesn't even remember me, it's been so long," her uncle said.

No hint of guilt in his voice. No shadow of doubt on his face.

She braced herself for him to touch her, but after advancing a few steps, he withdrew, dropping his arms to his sides. Now he searched her face with quick, darting eyes.

Fear!

In a flash of insight, Nina saw it revealed before he tucked it safely away.

He was afraid.

"We sure enjoyed having her stay with us, even though the circumstances were so unfortunate," her uncle said to her father.

"I was always grateful you were able to do it," her father said. Then he clapped his hands. "Nina, go tell Claire they're here. Or would you two like to go freshen up?"

"No, no," Aunt Elizabeth said. "We want to see you and the girls."

"I'll get Claire," Nina said. She climbed the stairs, still feeling a jumble of emotions. Part of her wondered if it had all been some hallucination on her part. How could her uncle stand there so calmly, knowing what he had done? Had that really been fear she'd seen in his innocent blue eyes? Or had he just picked up on her own tension?

She paused at the top landing. She had weathered the first encounter. But she was no nearer knowing what, if anything, she should do.

It was almost impossible to look at that dull, bland little man and see him as the man who had abused her so long ago. He had been a figure of nightmares for so long. Was this really the same person?

* * *

"So, how are your grades, Claire? This is your last year of high school, isn't it?"

Claire nodded. "My grades are fine. With any luck at all I'll be accepted to MIT next year."

Claire looked past her aunt's head and glared at Nina on the far side of the backyard. Nina was sitting by herself on one of the patio chairs, sipping a soda and by pointing her chair away from the others making it clear that she was not going to be involved in any way.

Typical Nina, Claire thought angrily. She had two modes for this kind of social occasion. She was either off in her own world or else driving everyone nuts with deliberately idiotic discussions. Frankly, right now Claire could have used the second Nina. Her aunt had been pestering her for the better part of an hour about guys, about school, about the island, about her plans, then back to guys. Meanwhile Uncle Mark seemed to have permanently attached himself to Mr. Geiger, nursing a bottle of beer and commenting on her father's handling of the grill.

"A climatologist? You mean like a weatherman on TV?"

"No, it's a little more involved than that," Claire said patiently.

Janelle bustled in and out of the house, screen door slamming, shuttling casserole dishes and napkins and pitchers of lemonade out to the table that had been set up in the middle of the yard. It was covered in a blue plaid tablecloth and set with plastic forks so there would be less cleanup.

185

Three of her father's employees from work, a man and two women, sat awkwardly by themselves, looking self-conscious about being at the boss's house. The neighbors, the Lafollettes, were due to come over any moment.

"Antarctica? Can't you study the weather somewhere nicer?"

"That's sort of the point. You study weather where there's lots of weather to study."

Suddenly Claire saw Nina jump up out of her chair. She trotted over to meet Zoey, who was coming around the side of the house, leading Benjamin.

Claire's stomach lurched. Oh, great. Perfect Nina touch, inviting the guy Claire had just recently broken up with. Wonderful. Now, if Jake showed up, as she hoped he would, the scene would be complete—the guy she had dumped but who still, probably, liked her, and the guy who had dumped her, who she definitely still liked.

Where was Lucas? He would make the crowning touch.

"MIT? Isn't that a boys'—"

"Excuse me, Aunt Elizabeth," Claire said, interrupting the latest question. "I have to go and play hostess for a moment."

Claire got up, feeling no relief as she traded one awkward situation for another. "Hi, Zoey, Benjamin."

"Claire," Benjamin said with his usual smug mockery, "I'll bet you're thrilled to see me here."

"Daddy will be glad," Claire said. "You know

186

you're his favorite choice for son-in-law. Or son, for that matter.''

Claire grabbed her sister's arm and pulled Nina aside. "Nice move. Do you realize I've invited Jake?'' she demanded in a whisper. "Me and Benjamin and Jake and Zoey?''

"Whatever,'' Nina said distractedly.

Claire sighed. "Do you always have to be a pain in the ass, Nina?''

Nina stared at her disconcertingly. Her eyes darted toward where their father and Uncle Mark were standing over the coals. Nina looked as if she were going to say something, but instead she just walked away quite suddenly, as if Claire didn't matter.

Benjamin was on Zoey's arm, since he wasn't familiar with the backyard. Aunt Elizabeth was introducing herself to them, peering closely at Benjamin's shades.

Benjamin was pulling one of his patented routines, Claire observed, trying unsuccessfully to keep herself from smiling. He was standing directly in front of her aunt, reaching to shake hands but deliberately aiming his hand far off to the side. When Aunt Elizabeth sidestepped to grab it he instantly turned in the other direction, forcing her to jump back.

"Are you a friend of Claire's, or of Nina's?'' Aunt Elizabeth asked him, still staring at his sunglasses like she was trying to look around them.

"I'm the family chauffeur,'' Benjamin said with a perfectly straight face.

"Oh, I . . . Oh."

Benjamin smiled.

"Oh, it's a *joke*," Aunt Elizabeth said, looking relieved. "I get it."

The back door of the house swung open and slammed back on its springs as Janelle reappeared, carrying a covered tray of rolls. Immediately behind her came Jake, carrying two flats of beer.

Claire smiled and went over to intercept him. "You came," she said with quiet satisfaction.

He shrugged with the heavy burden. "My dad said if I was coming, I should contribute some beer. He gave me a couple cases."

"You didn't have to," Claire said.

"Where should I put it?" Jake asked, still refusing to smile or give any sign that he was anything more than a casual guest.

"There's a big chest full of ice over there." She pointed.

"I'll go ice them down, then," Jake said.

He shifted his arms beneath his burden and Claire noticed something. The two cardboard flats held only six six-packs, not the eight that would make two cases.

Probably Jake had just misspoken. Probably it never had been two cases. Either that, or Jake had stashed two six-packs away for himself. In which case that might have been the only reason he'd come at all.

Eighteen

A platter of corn, passing down the table, chased by a dish of soft butter. A piece of swordfish on her plate, smelling of hickory smoke. Zoey's voice, quietly telling Benjamin the layout of his plate—steak, already cut, at six o'clock, beans at two o'clock, lemonade just up from his right hand. One of the people from her father's office trying to make conversation with Jake on the subject of the football team. A fork dropping onto the grass and old Mr. Lafollette bending over to pick it up because his wife's arthritis is too bad. A sudden burst of brittle laughter from Aunt Elizabeth.

Nina stares down at her plate, filled with food. She is starving and nauseous at the same time. She picks at the fish and takes a bite, chewing it as if it is rubber.

Conversation rises and falls around her, swelling to near enthusiasm, then ebbing, giving way to slurping and chewing sounds before picking up again.

She steals glances from under a lowered brow. Jake, acting as though no one will notice his Styrofoam cup is filled with beer and not lemonade. The three people from her father's job, falling into what is probably a very familiar ritual of talking among themselves about work, no longer so put off that the boss is sitting nearby. Claire, looking up at the sky as if she is praying for rain. She probably is. Her father, playing the role of genial host, trying to involve as many people as possible in the conversation, modestly accepting compliments for his skill with the coals.

Zoey is looking thoughtful, or perhaps just tired. And she is stealing looks down the table at Uncle Mark. Probably wondering whether this bland, ordinary-looking, middle-aged man in a short-sleeved plaid cotton shirt and silver-rimmed glasses could possibly be the man Nina had described. It's almost possible to see the doubt on Zoey's face, to read the thoughts—is Nina making it all up? Is it all some product of her overactive imagination? After all, this man looks so normal, and everyone knows Nina is not quite . . . quite.

Zoey looks at her. For a moment their eyes meet, and Nina is sure she reads guilt there. Guilt, because in her heart Zoey has begun to doubt.

Nina looks back down at her plate and drags her fork through the rapidly cooling beans. It's one thing to believe Nina's story in the abstract. It's another thing entirely to be sitting at the table with the man Nina has described as a child molester, a man who now seems so boringly ordinary.

She can't blame Zoey. She can't. After all, if the situation were reversed and it was Zoey pointing

190

the finger at a man who looked like the soul of innocence, would Nina believe unquestioningly?

His voice rises against a general lull. Even the voice is unthreatening. Not exactly Freddy Kreuger. Just a man a little intimidated by his brother-in-law's home, making self-deprecating references to the way the noise of the jets from the airport makes it hard for him to cook out in his own, much smaller backyard.

"It is *so* quiet here," Aunt Elizabeth says admiringly. "You must sleep so well at night, Burke."

"Not everyone can live on an island," Uncle Mark says, grinning to show he isn't envious. "Riding that ferry back and forth every day must be a pain in the ass. Living your life according to a schedule."

"It can be inconvenient," Mr. Geiger allows.

Of course, Nina's father rarely takes the ferry. He can afford to use the water taxi, but that would seem like boasting.

"Although with bankers' hours..." Uncle Mark says. "I mean, what is it, Burke, about a five-hour workday?" He laughs to show he's just kidding. Just ribbing his brother-in-law.

Nina's father turns it into a bigger joke. "Hell, Mark, I don't even work that much. I just leave the tellers to run the place. Isn't that right, Ellen?" he calls down the table to his head teller.

A plate of rolls appears, and Nina must pass it on. When she listens again, her uncle is saying in a low voice that the young blind boy certainly does

191

handle himself well. "You almost wouldn't guess, the way he can clean his plate," Mark says.

Nina feels a stiffening in her muscles. She is outraged. She wants to yell, *Don't you dare condescend to Benjamin! He's ten times the human being you'll ever be.*

But Benjamin, as usual, has a better way. Without acknowledging he has heard anything, he lifts his next forkful of fish and deliberately sticks it in his chin. He frowns and tries again, sticking it in his forehead.

Zoey, Claire, and Jake all stifle the urge to laugh, refusing to look at each other for fear they will lose control. Even Nina smiles at the memory they all share—the day Benjamin spent ten full minutes in the lunchroom trying to eat a spoonful of Jell-O. At first kids had thought it was for real. Then, one by one, they had caught on. People had laughed till they cried and fell out of their chairs.

Now her uncle Mark is staring. He has caught on immediately to Benjamin's little game and his cheeks are flushed with anger. He's being made fun of by a blind kid.

There! There, if Zoey would only look, she would see the true face of the man who hides behind pretty blue eyes and smudged glasses. Oh, he doesn't like being made fun of. No. Uncle Mark has no sense of humor about himself.

Benjamin takes a second bite, pops it effortlessly into his mouth. Uncle Mark looks away, smoothing over his fury, releasing it in another direction, telling Aunt Elizabeth in too loud a voice that she has a piece of food caught in her teeth.

Nina nods, feeling better. No need to be so afraid of a man who can be humiliated by Benjamin. Benjamin isn't afraid. She looks at Benjamin, inscrutable behind his shades. He's not a big, powerful guy like Jake. He's vulnerable to any sighted person who wants to walk up and take a punch at him. He should be afraid, always. Only he isn't.

She can survive this, she decides. She will keep her distance during the day and keep her door locked at night. In a few days it will be over and the monster will be gone again. He won't visit again soon, and in a couple of years she'll be gone from this house, at college, at work, in her own life where she will decide who has access. Then she will be done with him forever.

The conversation drops into another lull, this time deeper, more expectant. Nina listens. Her aunt is talking in a full, fruity voice, loaded with happy anticipation.

". . . never had children. It wasn't that we didn't want to. It was *me*," she adds quickly at a look from her husband. "I mean, *I* wasn't able."

"I was worried it might be me," Mark interjects, just in case anyone has missed the point, "but we got tested and it turned out I was fine."

"Anyway, we think now is the time to think about taking the big step. And we've been talking to an adoption agency . . ."

Nina feels her heart trip.

". . . and they have a little girl for us. She's not quite two years . . ."

Congratulations. Excellent news. This deserves a toast.

Nina sees Zoey, looking uncertain, worried. She sees Benjamin's lips pressed into a thin line. Nina feels dizzy, floating. She feels as if she might be fainting. Only she is still hearing the words. Her uncle's words now.

"I've always wanted a little girl of my own, ever since we had Nina stay with us all those years ago."

Nina's hand goes to her throat, her heart is banging in her chest, her breath coming in gasps.

No! No, no, no, no. He can't. He can't. He won't.

Before she realizes what she's doing, Nina stands up.

"Oh, my God," Zoey whispered under her breath.

Nina began to speak, but it was a low, hoarse whisper, indistinguishable above the babble of happy voices. She cleared her throat. Claire had stopped to look at her disapprovingly, obviously expecting some joke.

"I don't think you're going to adopt anyone," Nina said softly, tears coursing down her cheeks.

Several of the people closest to her fell silent, looking at her uncertainly. The silence spread down the table.

"Did you have something to say, Nina?" her father asked in a patient tone.

". . . yes."

In a flash Zoey saw it—the blood drained from Mark's face. His eyes went wide, then narrowed. He stared daggers at Nina.

Zoey could see Nina falter, but then she recovered herself. "I said, I don't think you're going to adopt anyone. Ever."

Her father winced good-naturedly. "Nina, I don't think this is the time for playing games. If you want to say congratulations . . ."

"I don't think they let child molesters adopt," Nina said. "At least, not in most states," she added, stiffly ironic.

"Nina, that's enough," her father rapped angrily.

"He likes little girls," Nina said through gritted teeth.

"Goddamnit, Nina that's more than enough!" her father shouted, his face darkening. "What is the matter with you?"

Mark was frozen in place, his face an unreadable, rigid mask.

"Nina, I don't think this is going to get a big laugh," Claire said.

Nina wavered. Zoey could see her flinch before her father's anger and her sister's scorn. Zoey wanted to say something, come to her defense, but what could she say? All she knew was what Nina had told her.

"Daddy," Nina said in a different, pleading

voice. "It's true. It's true. When I stayed with them . . . he . . ." She looked wildly around the table. "He . . . did things to me. At night he would come into my room and—" She was sobbing now.

"How long do I have to sit here and listen to this, Burke?" Mark snapped, suddenly alive again as he saw Nina weaken. "If you can't control your children—"

"Nina, leave this table at once," Mr. Geiger said in a menacing growl. "This is too much, even for you."

"But I'm telling the truth," Nina said in a whisper.

"No," her uncle said in a flat, utterly convincing voice. "You are not telling the truth."

For an eternity, thirteen people seemed to sit like statues, poised on the edge but unable to move one way or the other.

Then there was a new voice.

"Nina doesn't lie," Claire said.

"She *is* lying," Mark said. "Or else she thinks this is funny."

Claire shook her head. She stared coldly at her uncle. "No. I know Nina. This isn't a joke."

Mr. Geiger hesitated now, looking with new suspicion at his brother-in-law.

"Surely, Burke . . ." Aunt Elizabeth began.

Claire looked directly at her father. "I believe Nina."

Suddenly Zoey was speaking. "She told me a couple of days ago, Mr. Geiger. She spent last night at my house because she was afraid to face him. I believe her, too.''

"This is absurd and offensive," Mark said. "I've always known you didn't like me much, Burke, but I didn't think you'd let this sort of thing go on. I've been slandered in front of all these people. If this isn't stopped instantly, well, brother-in-law or not, I'll sue your butt.''

"Mark . . . Burke . . .'' Elizabeth pleaded.

"Shut up, Elizabeth," Mark snapped.

"Mr. G.,'' Benjamin said, "you have a choice here. You believe him, or you believe your daughter.''

"Burke, you know better,'' Elizabeth reasoned. "Do you think for one moment I would allow something like that to go on in my house? Do you?''

Mr. Geiger smiled sadly. He took his sister's hand gently. "Yes, sweetie. I'm afraid you would.'' He didn't look at Mark. "I can have you charged here in Maine, Mark, or you can catch the next ferry off the island and I'll have you charged back in Minnesota. Your choice. The next ferry leaves in thirty minutes.''

Mr. Geiger stood up, walked around the table, and put his arms around his younger daughter.

Nineteen

Nina knocked at the door to Claire's room. When there was no answer, she opened the door cautiously and went inside. "Claire? You in here?"

No answer, but when Nina looked up, she could see that the square hatchway that opened onto the widow's walk was open. She went over to the ladder and looked up at the patch of dark, star-strewn sky. "Claire?"

Claire's face appeared in the square, her long dark hair hanging down. "Oh, hi."

"Can I come up?" Nina asked.

"I can come down if you'd like," Claire said.

"No." Nina climbed the ladder till her head poked up through the hatchway into the cool night air. She leaned back against the opening, feet propped on a ladder rung. She had never gone out onto the widow's walk. The height made her nervous, and anyway, it was Claire's private turf. "It got colder."

"Yeah, there's a cold front moving in," Claire said, standing tall and looking off toward the mainland. "It's moving pretty fast, so we might get some nice storms. See, a cold front moves like a wedge beneath . . .'' She stopped herself. "Sorry. I don't guess you want a lecture on weather tonight.''

Nina shrugged. "I know you like a good storm.''

"These probably wouldn't last very long. Short but violent, if we get lucky.'' Claire sat down by the edge of the hatch. "You okay?''

"I had a talk with Dad.''

Claire waited patiently for her to go on.

"Lots of apologies and remorse and all,'' Nina said.

"Yeah, well, I owe you some of those myself,'' Claire said, looking away.

"No, you don't.''

"I should have . . . I don't know, I should have known, somehow.''

"I didn't tell you,'' Nina said. "I didn't tell anyone.''

Claire bit her lip. "I never exactly made it easy for you to talk to me.''

Nina smiled. "Claire, it's not easy for anyone to talk to you. You're kind of a difficult person. Unlike me, Ms. Normal of the Nineties.''

A fresher breeze lifted Claire's hair and rustled the top branches of the trees. Overhead the stars were obliterated by an advancing wave of cloud. "Definite storm,'' Claire said contentedly. "It'll be along soon now. I have to come down and get my poncho.''

Nina descended the ladder, with Claire right behind her. Claire grabbed the yellow rubber poncho from the hook on the back of her closet door and slipped it on.

199

"You look like the aftermath of a terrible accident involving a school bus," Nina commented.

Claire went toward the ladder, then stopped and turned back. "Look, Nina. I know we haven't ever been—"

"The Bobbsey twins?" Nina supplied.

"But you know, I am your sister. You could always tell me anything. I wouldn't laugh at you or give you a hard time."

Nina grinned. "Sure you would."

Claire made her rare, wintry smile. "Okay, but only at first."

Nina looked at her sister, lush dark hair under a crumpled plastic hat and draped over the shoulders of a bright yellow slicker. She was preparing to go up and sit in the middle of a thunderstorm. *And you're supposed to be the* normal *Geiger sister*, Nina thought.

A flash of lightning lit up the square in the ceiling. "You don't want to miss your storm," Nina said.

"It will be over soon, you know, if you want to talk or anything."

"I guess I'm going to start seeing your old shrink," Nina said. "She did such a fine job of turning you into a model citizen."

"Probably a good idea," Claire allowed. "Make up some good dreams for her. She loves a good, symbolic dream."

"Yeah, I can manage that," Nina said dryly. "Look, um . . . thanks, all right?"

"For what?"

"Things were on edge there, this afternoon. You backed me up."

Claire made a no-big-deal face. "I just said what I know. I just said you don't lie, not about the important things. Fortunately, no one asked me what I thought about the way you dress, or act, or your idiotic habit of sucking on unlit cigarettes."

"Idiotic," Nina echoed. "From the girl who's going to go sit in the rain." Nina hesitated, feeling an unfamiliar urge. "Jeez, I hate to do this. It's such a cliché." She held out her arms.

"Well, if we have to." Claire put her arms around Nina, and they hugged each other for a long time.

"When do we stop?" Nina asked.

"It's up to you," Claire said. "You're the one who started this."

"I'm thinking this is plenty long."

"On the count of three," Claire said.

"Three," Nina said.

They stepped back from each other, both looking awkward and embarrassed. Lightning flashed again, and Nina could see Claire counting off the distance, "One one thousand, two one thousand, three one thousand—"

The thunderclap rattled the windows.

"Don't get hit by lightning," Nina said.

"I've taken the appropriate safety measures."

"Yeah, you're a real model of common sense," Nina said sarcastically. "I hope I can grow up to be just like you."

"I'm still betting you never grow up," Claire grumbled as she climbed the ladder.

Nina

Over time, I've added a new dream. Number four. It incorporates many of the same images from the other dreams. In it I'm still a little girl wearing a dress with a ridiculously large bow on the front. And I'm still feeling myself drawn across an open floor toward a man with burning, terrible eyes.

And in the dream I'm still afraid. I don't know when that will go away. I know it will someday, but I don't know when.

Only now there's something new. I feel someone else in the

dream with me. And I know, as you sometimes just know things in dreams, that this other person is on my side.

When I wake up, I wonder who this other person is. Zoey? Benjamin? Then I realize it's both of them, somehow. Them, and a little of my father, and a lot of my big sister, Claire.

They can't protect me from the man with burning eyes, or from the fear, but because they are there I no longer feel the shame.

Twenty

"How can you blame me?" Lucas demanded for the hundredth time. "I did my best to *lose*. I called everyone I know. I called people I didn't know. No one could have tried harder to lose than I did."

He was trailing just a few steps behind Zoey, who was marching down the street from school to the homeward-bound ferry Monday afternoon. Nina marched beside Zoey and Aisha in solidarity, although frankly, Nina could see Lucas's point. It wasn't really his fault he had been voted homecoming king. It was funny, but it wasn't his fault.

"If I could find a way to quit without offending everyone in the entire student body, I would," he said.

"You and Louise Kronenberger." Zoey snarled the name. "You and dial-a-slut."

"It's not my fault I won, and it's not my fault you came in . . . that you didn't win."

"Third," Zoey said. "I believe what you were going to say is that I came in third. Not even runner-up, while you, Mr. I'm-Too-Good-for-All-This-Juvenile-Stuff, Mr. Tough Guy, Mr. Way Too

Cool, you win. *You* win." She threw up her hands.

Nina looked over her shoulder at Lucas. "You thoughtless bastard," she said, mimicking Zoey's tone.

"It's just a dumb contest," Lucas said. "You yourself said you lost student council last year to Butthead."

Zoey spun around. "I did not lose to Butthead. I *beat* Butthead, I'll have you know, by eight votes."

"Yeah, she lost to Beavis, you insensitive jerk," Aisha said, giving Nina a wink that avoided Zoey's notice.

"K-berger," Zoey said. "She's slept with every guy in school already."

"Well, she hasn't slept with me yet," Lucas grumbled. He winced, and sucked air in through his teeth. "I mean—"

"Too late, Lucas," Nina advised, shaking her head sadly. "Now you're really in trouble."

"Tell him he can do whatever he wants with the homecoming queen," Zoey said to Nina. "Tell him he's the homecoming king, after all."

"She says if you so much as look at Louise Kronenberger, you're a dead man," Nina interpreted.

"Tell him I'm sure I'll find *someone* who's willing to take me to the homecoming game and dance, since my alleged boyfriend will be busy," Zoey said.

"I'll take this one," Aisha said. "Lucas, Zoey plans to find a really great-looking, possibly rich, probably older date who will make you feel absolutely insecure, so that your whole night will be ruined thinking that she may be off making out with him."

Lucas reached out both hands and grabbed Nina and Aisha by their shoulders. He pulled both girls to a halt. Zoey went marching on obliviously. "You two stay out of this," Lucas said.

He broke into a trot and went after Zoey.

"He's so forceful and manly," Aisha said mockingly.

"Twenty seconds to major lip lock," Nina predicted.

"He's not that fast, and Zoey will mess with him for at least another minute," Aisha said.

Nina held her arm up so that both could see her watch.

"She's stopped," Nina said.

"Come on, Zoey," Aisha muttered.

"Boom," Nina announced. "Twenty-four seconds."

"Damn."

"By the way, Eesh, it *was* you who started the move to nominate Lucas, wasn't it?" Nina asked.

"Of course. Just don't ever tell Lucas or Zoey. I thought they'd both win."

"That was very romantic of you," Nina said as they resumed their walk. "I didn't think that was your style."

"It won't be again," Aisha said. "You see how well this worked out."

*　　*　　*

"Down, forty-two, hut, HUT."

The ball snapped and Jake sprang forward. One step, sharp left turn, see the ball in the quarterback's hand, grab, tuck, right turn, there's a hole!

He ran. Two yards, three yards, first down and nothing in his way—

Something like a truck hit him from out of nowhere and he went flying. He hit the grass on his back, gasping for air, but still holding the ball. He was staring up at the clear blue sky when the grinning face of his teammate appeared above him, hand outstretched.

"Didn't hurt you, did I?" Mark Simpson asked.

"Didn't hurt *me*," Jake said, grinning ruefully. "But if you hit the running back from Bath like that next week, we might just win our homecoming game for once."

Mark slapped him on the back. "Hey, your girl is over there again."

"What girl?" Jake asked.

"What girl?" Mark echoed, not convinced. "I think you know what girl. But look, man, if you don't want her . . ."

"She's too smart to go out with a lousy lineman," Jake said.

"That's it for today, ladies!" the coach yelled out. "Hit the showers. And, uh, McRoyan?"

"Yeah, coach?" Jake answered.

"Keep *both* your eyes open and you don't get hit so often."

Jake gave a genial raised finger to the rest of the team, which laughed appreciatively at his expense.

He began to trot back to the gym, but he lagged behind as if some invisible power were pulling him backward. He stopped and watched the rest of the team run on ahead. He turned. Claire was still there, sitting on the bleachers.

He looked at her, a lonely, exquisitely beautiful figure. She drew him like the gravity of a black hole might draw a passing comet. What did she want with him? Was it all just guilt, or was there really something more?

And did it matter? Despite all his vows to himself and to the memory of Wade, he had allowed her to help him when he needed help. He had gone to that disastrous barbecue the day before. And he wanted to go to her now.

They were looking at each other across a hundred feet of grass and too many memories. If he ran to her now, it would all be over. He would have betrayed Wade at last.

He began to walk, pulling off his helmet as he went. She came down from the bleachers, graceful, perfect. He took her in his arms. Her lips opened to him.

Wade had always said he was weak. Maybe Wade was right.

But he wasn't as weak as Claire thought he was.

He pushed her away. Not roughly, gently. Then he walked away and didn't look back.

Nina wandered around the familiar deck of the ferry, enjoying the cool crisp air of Claire's cold front. The storms had swept through and left the world washed and newly perfumed. A pair of harbor seals were playing in the wake of the boat, diving and reappearing, staring in bemusement at the humans who were smiling down at them.

She sat down next to Benjamin. He had earphones on, some faint music escaping in wisps. For a while she looked at him. He was just a few feet away but unaware of her presence. *Pretty much as usual*, she thought ruefully. *Pretty much the way it's always been.*

She reached over and raised one earphone. "What are you listening to?"

"Music," Benjamin said. He switched off his Walkman and pulled down the earphones so that they hung around his neck.

"Don't ask me," Nina warned.

"Don't ask you what?"

"Don't ask me how I'm doing. Zoey's asked me how I'm doing. Jake asked me. Aisha asked me. Lucas. Tad Crowley. Two teachers and a cafeteria worker. The entire world is very concerned with how I'm doing."

"News travels fast," Benjamin said. "They're just trying to be nice."

"I know. It's getting on my nerves big time. I feel like I'm walking around with a neon sign on my head that says *victim*. I'm not weird, strange, out-there Nina anymore. Now I'm poor Nina."

Benjamin nodded. "Tell me about it."

"I'm supposed to start seeing the all-purpose shrink. I hear you're not allowed to graduate anymore unless you've had at least one major psychological problem requiring professional help.''

"It's very fashionable," Benjamin agreed. "Have you considered going on *Oprah* and turning your private life into entertainment for half the country?''

"I want to do *Montel*. It's much sleazier. But actually, you know, I happen to be acquainted with someone who is the world's best expert at getting people to treat you like you're normal.''

Benjamin grinned. "It's all an act.''

"It doesn't look like an act," Nina said sincerely. "I've never seen you feel sorry for yourself, never once.''

"Well, you want to catch me sometime in the middle of the night. Around three or four when I wake up and I can't get back to sleep. I lie there just making lists of all the jobs I'll never be able to have, and all the great places and things I'll never see. I imagine the day when I'll be walking down the street and some guys will come up and realize how helpless I really am and beat the crap out of me.''

"I didn't know you did that," Nina said sadly.

"I've had a pretty good share of bitterness. Try having a dream sometime where you can see, see everything perfectly and then . . . wake up, and see nothing.'' He forced a wry smile. "God, now I'm even depressing myself.''

"Well, we're sitting in the Depressed Losers section," Nina said.

"Are we? Damn. I meant to sit in the Giddy Optimists section.''

"How could you know? You're blind," Nina pointed out.

Benjamin nodded. "You'll do okay, Nina. People will get past it. Soon you'll just be weird, strange, out-there Nina again. In the meantime, screw it. You can't let the pity get to you."

"I know you never did," Nina said.

Benjamin sighed, then smiled. "I did my best to make pity impossible."

"The Jell-O," Nina said, chuckling. "Classic. You made me blow milk through my nose. Or how about the girls' locker room when the cheerleaders were all in there?"

Benjamin laughed. "Yes, I'm the happy blind guy," he said with just a trace of irony. "I always figure, hell, if people are going to feel sorry for you, you have to surprise them. They think they know what you are and how you must feel. So I always try to keep them guessing. Do the thing no one expects you to do—like make fun of the way you can't eat very gracefully, or make people think you've somehow found a way to turn things to your advantage. There are guys who still think somehow, they don't know how, but *somehow* I got a look at all the cheerleaders naked."

"People admire you," Nina said sincerely. "No one's said poor Benjamin in a long time."

"I don't think anyone exactly admires me," Benjamin scoffed.

"I do," Nina said before she could think about it and stop herself. "I think you're an amazing person."

211

Benjamin actually seemed to be blushing. For once he was at a loss for words. "Oh, it's . . . don't . . ."

"And you know what else?" Nina said with sudden recklessness.

"What?"

Now a lump rose in her throat, threatening to choke her. "Well . . ." she began lamely, swallowing hard. "I . . . I kind of . . . you know, I like you." She ended in a mutter and immediately buried her face in her hands. She peeked through her fingers. Benjamin's brow was wrinkled.

"Really?"

Nina took a deep breath. "Look, it's no big deal. It's just that I happen to think you're a cool guy and all."

"So, it's not like you're—"

"Yes!" Nina said, exploding. "Yes, that's exactly what it's like, Benjamin. You know, you're not just blind, you're dense. If you could see, you'd still be blind. I don't know why I do like you, because you are the biggest dolt on earth sometimes."

"So . . . So, you want to go out?"

"Duh."

"How about homecoming? I don't have a date."

"Okay, I'll go out with you, but it's not going to be like when we went to that concert in Portland and you acted like I was your chauffeur for the evening."

Benjamin smiled impishly. "No one would expect to see you and me at the dance together."

"I always figure, hell, if people are going to feel sorry for you, you have to surprise them," Nina quoted his words back to him.

"You know, dancing with a blind guy can be dangerous."

"That's okay," Nina said. "When you touch me, I'll probably get hysterical."

"Then it's a date."

"Yes," Nina said. "It's a date."

Twenty-one

Aisha said good-bye to Zoey and Lucas at Zoey's house and started the climb uphill to her home. She had just reached the first big turn when she changed her mind. If she went home right away, her mother would probably draft her into some cleanup or fix-up chore, which, on top of her homework, would pretty well kill the night.

And it was Monday. On Monday nights Passmores' closed now, which meant Christopher wouldn't be cooking.

She took the turn that led back to Leeward Drive. Maybe Christopher would be home, maybe not. But she'd rather spend time with him than go straight home. Their date Saturday had been the most romantic evening of her life. And it had been followed by Sunday, when they had gone swimming together down at the pond. Far from making her feel that she had seen enough of him for a while, their time together seemed to have had the opposite effect.

Too bad he wasn't still in school. Too bad he worked so much. She had to get an hour of him here and a few hours there. "It's official, girl," she told herself. "You've got it big time."

Maybe she should tell Christopher how she felt now. She never had, and he'd never asked her. At least, neither of them had spoken the dreaded *L*-word.

It would probably scare him to death, Aisha thought. He'd probably think she was crazy.

But on the other hand, he might feel the same way himself.

Aisha savored that possibility, turning it over in her mind. If she said it first, maybe he would say it, too.

Although it would be better still if he said it first. That way she wouldn't face the possibility that he would just look at her with his mouth gaping and stammer.

She walked along the road, energized by the coolness of the late afternoon. The beach to her right was half-devoured by high tide, and the sun was already dropping precipitously toward the horizon. The days shortened early in Maine. Soon it would be dark as night by five.

She reached the ramshackle Victorian and, now familiar with the routine, went on inside and up the stairs, humming with anticipation.

Maybe she would tell him, and maybe she wouldn't. Maybe she would wait for him to be the first. It was a dumb game, but then, she had abandoned all pretense to being sensible where Christopher was concerned.

She knocked on his door. There was a sound

inside, and her heart leapt happily. He was home.

Aisha straightened her hair with a quick swipe of her hand just as the door opened.

He stood there in shorts and no shirt, and Aisha decided right then and there—she loved him. She should tell him and to hell with games.

"Hi," she said, smiling.

"Aisha," he said in a low whisper.

She stood on her toes to kiss him, but he pulled back. Over his shoulder Aisha saw a movement.

She searched his eyes, which had gone opaque and evasive.

"This isn't a good time," Christopher said. "I didn't know you were coming over."

Again the flash of movement, and now Aisha could see more clearly as the girl with impossibly long blond hair rolled off Christopher's bed and stood up.

Making Out: Ben's in Love

Book 4 in the explosive series about broken hearts, secrets, friendship and, of course, love.

First **Zoey** fooled around with **Lucas** and **Jake** found out. Then **Claire** wanted **Jake,** so she broke up with **Ben** but ended up alone. Now **Nina** is in love with **Ben** and **Claire** wants **Ben** back. Will **Claire** try to steal her ex-boyfriend back from her own sister?

Ben's In Love